GREY SAGE

Center Point
Large Print

**This Large Print Book carries the
Seal of Approval of N.A.V.H.**

GREY SAGE

Francis W. Hilton

CENTER POINT LARGE PRINT
THORNDIKE, MAINE

This Center Point Large Print edition is published
in the year 2017 by arrangement with
Golden West Literary Agency.

First US edition: H. C. Kinsey & Company.
First UK edition: Rich & Cowan.

The text of this Large Print edition is unabridged.
In other aspects, this book may vary
from the original edition.
Printed in the United States of America
on permanent paper.
Set in 16-point Times New Roman type.

ISBN: 978-1-68324-386-1 (hardcover)
ISBN: 978-1-68324-390-8 (paperback)

Library of Congress Cataloging-in-Publication Data

Names: Hilton, Francis W., author.
Title: Grey sage / Francis W. Hilton.
Description: Center Point Large Print edition. | Thorndike, Maine :
Center Point Large Print, 2017.
Identifiers: LCCN 2017003833| ISBN 9781683243861 (hardcover :
alk. paper) | ISBN 9781683243908 (pbk. : alk. paper)
Subjects: LCSH: Large type books. | GSAFD: Western stories.
Classification: LCC PS3515.I6983 G74 2017 | DDC 813/.52—dc23
LC record available at https://lccn.loc.gov/2017003833

GREY SAGE

Chapter I

Vast acres lay about him—acres parched and cracked with heat, clotted with bunch-grass and sage, that spread out in a great dun-coloured floor to hazy horizons—untillable, sterile acres worthless save for the herds that still roamed the alkali wastes of Northeastern Wyoming.

Limitless was that expanse. It danced and swayed like a mirage in the shimmering heat, the only life a bunch of cattle trailing dustily in search of water. A cluster of abandoned shacks stood lonely vigil, mute evidence of the struggle of some homesteader forced to sacrifice the fruitless toil of years and move on to start anew. Storm-blackened boards with staring yellow pitch-knots, like sightless eyes, curled on the barns and outbuildings. Rank weeds choked the dooryard, packed hard by hoofs of prowling stock that had huddled beneath the sagging roof for shade or warmth. Tumble-weeds, stacked for feed during leaner years when the pitiless sun completely denuded the soil, lay in matted heaps; tumble-weeds rolled lazily across the cow-trails in the slow, hot June wind, to pile up against barbed wire that drooped dejectedly from rotting fence-posts.

On a mesa, looking down on the great sweep of prairie-land, the cowboy hunkered to drag on a cigarette. Close by, bridle-reins trailing, his pony snipped at tufts of withered grass with the optimism of animals born to the range. The cowboy smoked nervously, the fingers of one hand spinning a thin rowel of long-shanked spurs on booted heels. His overalls, skin-tight across lean hips and long legs, were powdered with dust. Dust covered his blue shirt, open at the throat to reveal a neck bronzed by wind and sun. Glistening particles of alkali clung to the stubble on his young, wind-whipped face, rimmed the crown of the battered hat pushed back from his forehead.

Troubled grey eyes looked out from beneath sunburned brows to trace the argent ribbon that twisted away towards the west—the Cheyenne River, flanked by straggling cottonwoods, their trunks scarred and glaring as the alkali beds that shone like upturned mirrors in the sun.

Beyond the river lay a patch of green, one oasis in the blistered land. It gave promise of water— a promise seen in the scattered cottonwoods, but not fulfilled by the dry and dusty beds of creeks and washes.

His homestead, that oasis. All his life he had wanted it—wanted to know the pride of possession and achievement, to feel himself a substantial part of this great range-land that gripped and held the souls of men. Always he had felt its strange spell. Even as a boy on his father's small ranch—especially on hot days when sultry breezes carried a tang of sage that seemed to stir his blood, or on moonless summer nights when brilliant stars hung low in the heavens, a canopy seemingly no more vast and limitless by night than the prairie reaches by day. He had felt it at sunset when misty purple shadows stretched long over the land and the dying sun laid plaits of gold on the dun-coloured earth.

Now the homestead was his—this thing he had always wanted. A fenced section with a spring; a rough two-room log cabin, a lean-to barn for his saddle-horse. Once he had attained them, had thrilled to their creation and possession, he had found in reality they meant little. Still something for which he longed was lacking. What it was he did not know. But it kept him prowling, always looking forward expectantly, hopefully.

Cold and unappreciative he had grown of the crude buildings, the drab prairie acres to the attainment of which, since boyhood, he had dedicated his life. At times he almost hated it. Those were the times when as now he sat to stare off across the flats with unseeing eyes, motionless as rock that littered the washes. He was under the spell of surging emotion which seemed to stifle him, leave him prey to that unquenchable longing he never could satisfy. Out there beyond the setting sun he seemed to glimpse that for which his soul cried; there he was sure he would find happiness, contentment, success.

Rousing himself presently, he crushed the fire from his cigarette, ground it beneath his heel—an ever-present precaution in range-land, where a single careless spark turned lifeless acres into livid, hissing walls of flame and smoke. Securing the bridle-reins of his pony, he swung into the saddle with an easy, graceful movement. He headed down off the mesa, turned towards the glinting river.

The trail ran yellow into the face of the lowering sun, a huge dusty serpent writhing in and out among the breaks. The silence was that of deathly places, a vast and palpitating silence that sometimes seemed to choke him, sometimes to soothe his violent moods. The only sounds that met his ears were the thin small sounds of Nature: the eerie whine of the breeze in the ravines; the swift thudding of a cotton-tail scuttling to cover in a grottoed bank; the whir of a rattler disturbed from a lazy sun-bath; the clacking of grass-hoppers.

Where the river crooked a roily arm about a towering gumbo cliff he reined off the trail and got down. He dropped a wire gate. Leading his pony through, he remounted and rode on. A short distance and he drew up before a tar-papered shack huddled beneath the overhanging bluff.

"Light, Grey," came a cheery greeting from the doorway—"light and stay for a snack. Just cooking up some victuals for supper."

"Howdy, Mason." For all the young strength of the cowboy there was something tired, something lifeless in his tone. "Reckon I'll do just that. If you don't mind, I'll stable my horse. May be wanting him."

"Leaving us?" Mason, a grizzled old cowhand with a tousled shock of iron-grey hair, faded blue eyes and weather-pitted face set off by a scraggly moustache, came limping from the shack as the cowboy turned into the sod-roofed barn. A crooked willow cane supported his weight—did poor service for a leg that hung stiffly from his hip: the lifelong brand of a horseman who had lost one savage encounter.

"I say . . ."—he stopped to brace himself while he pared a slice of tobacco from a dirty plug and rammed it into his cheek—". . . be you leaving, Grey?" He tongued the bitter morsel pleasantly.

"I don't know." The young cowboy slipped the bridle from his horse. It nosed the dusty hay in the manger disgustedly, turned to nicker for grain. "A man might just as well be dead as here. I'm sick of it all, Mason—sick of the heat and flies and stinking water-holes, cattle dying of thirst in the summer, starving and freezing in the winter. I want to do something . . . be something."

The old man chuckled. But there was no merriment in the sound. It was a harsh, dry cackle, like a muttered curse.

"And you, Grey Sage?" He hobbled over to

11

dump a scant measure of grain into the manger-box. The cowboy dragged the saddle from the pony's sweaty back, wiped the lather fringing the damp blanket from the brute's ribs. "The thing your paw loved more than anything else . . . and you wanting to leave it? That's why he named you Grey Sage. Your maw was ag'in it. She hated the grey sage as much as your paw loved it. She hated the country. And it got her."

"You never told me." The cowboy looked up accusingly. "What of my mother?"

"I wasn't aiming to tell you, ever." The pony fed, the old cowman took the youth by the arm, started back towards the shack. "But somehow when I saw your face as you rode up, heard you say you might be leaving, I just couldn't help it. You reminded me so much of your maw. She . . . she just pined away."

"Wasn't my father—"

"One of the finest men who ever lived," old Mason said. The catch in his voice was suddenly as old and tottery as his body—a catch that somehow reminded the younger man of the pitiful lowing of thirst-crazed cattle. "But your paw was a Westerner, born and raised on the range. No finer cowhand ever lived, the greatest rider ever to throw a leg across a bronc on the Cheyenne River."

"But my mother?"

"Your father was the world of kindness to her.

She was everything to him. Just a little flower reared in the East, refined, educated. She loved him and she stuck. The country got her, kid—this great big country that gets under your hide and chokes you with its bigness. She couldn't take it, any more than half the other women who try it out here in the sage-brush. It's hell on women and broncs.

"But . . . the day you were born. It was late summer. The sage was turning grey. The minute your paw saw you he says, sort of soft-like: 'Grey . . . that's the name to go with Sage, maw . . . our little shaver will be Grey Sage.'

"There was a hurt look came into your maw's eyes. I'd seen it time and again—a look of fear, like a crippled antelope that has quit the bunch and crawled into the brush to die alone. Not fear of your paw . . . fear for you . . . fear of the country.

" 'Not Grey Sage, Sam,' she whispered. 'He's so sweet and rolly-polly . . . Grey Sage is so dismal, so awful!' "

"But Grey Sage it was," the youth put in heavily.

"And the same grey sage that gave you your name covered her grave three months later. Grey Sage! How your paw loved it! How your poor little maw hated it! So you're going away, kid?"

But now they had entered the shack—a single room in which was a red-rusted camp stove, a

13

rough board table, a bed-roll, two benches. A barn-sash let into the dismal interior the dying light of the June sun, reflected it blindingly in a broken piece of mirror propped above a battered tin wash-basin in a corner. A few pictures clipped from the magazines that found their way into the river-country were tacked on the walls. Mostly of women they were—the one bright thing in the lonely life of isolated cowmen. Faded and torn, they still lent a touch of colour to the rough, smoke-blackened boards. From the stove came the rancid odour of burning grease, slopped from the spider in which potatoes were frying.

"Sometimes I think I'll go crazy out there on that homestead alone, doing nothing worth while, never amounting to a damn. I get to thinking . . . it's so damned lonesome. . . ." The youth sank on a bench to prop his chin in his hands, rub the stubble on his face.

"That's your maw in you." Old Mason hobbled over to stir the potatoes. He spilled some on the stove, placed them, piece by piece, back in the spider. "She tried to make herself like it . . . tried to be happy. She couldn't take it, any more than you can, kid. It's the country. It's getting you just like it got her, because you never see anything only the burned flats and the dismal grey bluffs, floods, heat, flies. It's too big for a man alone. The world always seems to be closing in on him, trying to crush him."

"But you have stayed."

"I never knew anything else—nor my mother didn't, either. My folks have lived right here in shacks along the river for sixty years. The strain in me that knew other places is too far back for me to feel. You inherited your mother's longing for the life she once knew—inherited her hate of the sage-brush country, her ambition to do big things."

The cowboy groaned.

"God, how it hurts when you're lonesome! That's why I want to get away."

"You'll come back," Mason prophesied. "That'll be your paw in you. He loved this country. You love it too. Better than you'll ever know until you get to where you can't smell and see this grey sage any more, where you can't feel the bigness of things about you, where you seem sort of close-penned . . . like a range critter first run into a corral."

"I know I'll miss it. For even when I'm lone-somest there's something deep inside me that's sort of happy. That's why I came to you. Some-times I don't think I can stand it another day. Then, when I get out in the brush—"

The old man stopped him with a gnarled hand on his shoulder.

"I know, kid. Get away from it. It'll be good for you. Get out among people . . . out where you can see something besides starving critters and stinking water-holes. When you finally decide to come back, bring a wife with you."

"And let her die as my mother died?"

"Get a woman of the West, a girl who knows this big country, one who loves the brush. Don't ever marry a woman who doesn't. You'll only wreck her life and your own."

"There'll be plenty of time for that," listlessly. "But what'll I do out there? I haven't any education. All I know is horses and cattle. I want to be somebody, I tell you."

"A man who knows one thing good will get by better than the fellow who knows a lot of things half-way. You know horses. No finer rider ever stepped across a bronc—unless it was your dad. Your mother gave you the longing to get out of the brush. Your paw gave you the one thing that is going to take you out. How long have you been breaking horses for the ranchers hereabouts?"

"Since I can remember."

"Ever afraid of a horse?"

"No."

"Still you say you can't do anything. You've got a job, kid . . . a big job for the rest of your life."

"Riding?"

"Yes, in rodeos. Get out there among them. Do the work your paw taught you to do—for money . . . big money. Go out there knowing you

16

can do it with the best of them. Ride . . . ride the worst of their broncs. Come out of those chutes knowing you'll win. That's the spirit your maw bred in you . . . the spirit that never broke until this damned sage—"

"Do you really think I can do it?"

"It ain't what I think. It's what you think. If you think you can, you can. Me . . . I know it. Here"—he scooped the potatoes into a cracked dish, caromed it across the oilcloth-covered table, tossed out a few slices of home-made bread—"throw some grub into you. We'll just auger this thing."

Chapter II

They sat in silence for a time. Mason wolfed the frugal meal. Grey Sage made but a poor attempt at eating.

"It's all so new to me," Grey essayed presently. "I don't know anything about rodeos . . . don't even know how to go about getting into them. I've never been to a place bigger than Merino. It's got two hundred people, and is only fifty miles from where I was born and raised."

"And you're twenty-two years old," scornfully. "My, my, you really should have been round the world at that age. Hell, lots of jaspers who go out and knock them dead never even went that fifty miles to Merino before they pulled up stakes and made good." He leaned over to punctuate his remarks with an upraised knife, a convincing light in his faded blue eyes. "It ain't the distance you've travelled, kid. It ain't what you've seen. It ain't where you were raised or how. It's how much, by God, you can produce of what they want that will get you by in this old world."

"I'm not afraid of their horses, or anything like that," Grey said. "I'm sort of scared of people. Kind of makes me skittish to think of getting away from where I know everybody and trying to bust in among strangers. Yet, I've got to do something besides this. But it takes money to go into rodeo contests. The boys over at the Running M told me there were entrance fees. If I just knew something about what I was getting into."

Mason shifted his crippled leg from beneath the table.

"Nobody recklects when I got that. But it was my first try at rodeo bronc-riding. I busted up for life at Cheyenne. That's why I asked if you were ever afraid of horses."

Grey did not so much as glance at the leg.

"The answer still is No."

"Guts is all it takes. If you ever get afraid, quit. Then is when a cowboy gets hurt."

"But, I never even saw a rodeo."

"Never saw a rodeo?" disgustedly. "Hell, you've ridden 'em since you were knee-high to a grasshopper. A rodeo is just another word for round-up."

"But they don't hold round-ups in the cities."

"Nothing less. The only difference is you don't have to do any night-herding or hawking. You don't roll out before dawn and work till after dark. You get paid money, have an honest-to-God bed to sleep in and good food to eat."

"Do people really pay to see what a cowboy does for a living?" incredulously.

"Thousands of 'em . . . and screech their heads off. Like they used to in the Roman circus we've read about. They put gladiators in the arena against each other . . . sometimes lions and gladiators. Now it's cowboys against horses and critters.

"The gladiator was on his own. If he got hurt, it was his look-out. To-day, if the cowboy gets crippled, that's his look-out, too. If you're killed . . . well, as the feller says, you only have to die once. Some day they'll have some protection for the rodeo cowboy—mebbeso a home, where he can go if he's hurt and won't have to spend his life trying to make a living with one leg dragging, like I've done."

"It ain't being afraid of getting hurt that scares me."

"I know. It's can you do it? That's the question every kid asks. It's the question men ask. It's the big question of the world. Don't let it worry you. Don't wonder if you can do it. Take the time you'd waste worrying and go ahead and do it.

"Now there's the entering. You have to sign up for bronc-riding, bareback-riding, steer-roping and the like. Each event costs an entrance fee."

"How much?"

"Oh, mebbeso ten dollars apiece. What you put out in entrance fees is given back in the purses at most shows. But there isn't any sense in you just entering the bronc-riding. You can throw a rope like nobody's business. You can wrestle your steer and tie it with the best of them. Don't you see, kid, you're there and over when it comes to knowing the stuff they pay to see at a rodeo?"

The youth pushed aside the uninviting food.

"I wonder if I could do it?"

"Your maw didn't wonder. Do you think for a minute she'd be wondering now if it meant something better for you? No, by God, she wouldn't. She'd be doing it, like she did when she came out here in the sage-brush to live and die—die with the lonesomeness that's going to get you too, if you don't shag it out of here. It don't make any difference where you're from. It's guts that puts you across. There ain't no question in my mind. Your maw would want you to do it . . . to see the things out there she died longing for. Your paw would want you to do it . . . to carry on the life he loved."

Grey Sage rose from the table. He strode to the open door, stood staring out in the purple dusk.

"But it takes money," he said slowly. "I haven't a dime since I put that round-up pay into crop. I'm barely eating. If it wasn't for cotton-tails, I'd be—"

"That's where friends fit in, kid." Mason stopped him. "Friends that can't be used in the pinches aren't worth a tinker's damn. I've got fifty dollars there in that tobacco can above the stove. Been saving it for a time when I could give somebody a lift like some of them gave me. Your maw, for instance."

21

"My mother?"

"Yes." Old Mason rose, limped over, secured the can. With gnarled fingers he pulled forth five dirty ten-dollar bills. "I loved your maw, kid. She never knew it, because she loved your paw. That's why I never married—'cause I never could see anybody that quite graded up with her. But"—he shook his tousled head sadly—"she just wasn't for me. Some day you may run across another man's wife that you'll love. If you ever do, play the game fair, like you play it with a bronc. Don't ever steal—whether it's a man's critters or his wife. It's all the same. They belong to him, and not to you." He came over to drop an arm about the youth's sagging shoulders and press the crumpled bills into his hand.

"Take them," he said huskily. "Shag on down to Arapahoe. Get into those stampede contests. Get out there and kick all the hair off of every bronc they snake in. Show 'em you can do it even if you never were more than fifty miles away from home before. The time will come when you run across a girl. Be sure she's a girl of the West. Then if you and her come back to the sage-brush you'll be happy. But don't come back until you've shown the whole world that they grow men with guts here in this lonesome hellhole we call the prairie country."

"I'm going to do it, Mason," the cowboy said. "You're giving me my chance. I'm coming back here some day the champion bronc-rider of the world."

"You'll do it too, kid, when you say it thataway." Old Mason's voice broke strangely. "All hell can't whip a Sage when he bows his neck. Do it, kid, for me . . . and for your maw.

"Champion bronc-rider of the world!" His faded eyes beamed. "Damn me, if you do it, I'll . . . well, I'll be ready to cash in my chips, because I'd have seen everything worth while in this world."

Chapter III

Grey Sage climbed the chute—awkwardly in his high-heeled boots, spur-rowels jangling. Knees braced against the top plank, he paused, batwing chaps emphasizing the slight bow of his long legs, shirt bellied out by the wind that chased dust over the Arapahoe rodeo-field and sifted it into the faces of watching thousands. Yet Grey was only vaguely conscious of those crowds that packed the grand-stand directly opposite and the bleachers at either end of the arena. The sea of faces ran in a blurred and jagged line across his vision. The roar of the throng was no more than a pulsing in his ears.

His gaze, his thoughts were all for a great bay horse tight-penned beneath him. The animal was lunging, trying to climb the gate, coming down to beat its head savagely against the sides of the chute. Cursing, sweating hostlers fought to catch with a hook the latigo dangling beneath its belly.

Grey Sage was the centre of interest in Arapahoe: not only because he had bucked into the finals and was a favourite to win a world championship, but also because he was a stranger. Strange riders with his ability—and especially clean-cut, good-looking ones such as he—were by no means common at any rodeo, and always drew considerable conjectures and surmise. Save for the managers, who had accepted his entrance fees, and who, unfortunately, had found no time to disseminate information concerning him, no one knew from whence he had come. The broad-shouldered, hipless cowboy had ridden into town on the eve of the big annual stampede. For all the shabbiness of the once-fancy-stitched boots, thorn-scarred chaps and battered hat, Cowland marked him by the curvetting horse he rowelled through the boisterous crowds. To the practised eye of cow-folk, who filled the Wyoming town to overflowing, at least six brands were visible on the sorrel coat of the terrified gelding. That meant but one thing to range-land. The horse, which had changed hands six times, either was a brute of great value, or was so savage no owner cared to keep him. By its eyes, skinned back to the whites, its ears, one up, one down, and its mincing movement under tight rein, it was evident that fear of the wrenching bit was all that kept it from burying its head and going sky-high.

Once he had cared for his mount, Grey Sage had quickly become a part of the crowd, moving about with graceful, easy strides, his silence as grim as his thin lips, forever pursed as in deep thought. While he had taken no part in the ear-splitting merriment that rocked the old frontier town, it was apparent that little had escaped his grey eyes—cold and sinister as the grey of a battleship, those eyes, and somehow, one sensed, fully as deadly.

Now, from the top of the chute, those eyes were fixed on the lunging bronc. Fearlessly they looked down upon the bawling, heaving brute. Yet deep within them gleamed a spark of uncertainty which might have come from spring-tight nerves. For all his uneasy manner, his movements were singularly cool, deliberate, almost careless.

After many futile attempts, the hostlers had caught the whipping latigo, run it through the cinch-buckle. They had jerked tight the saddle. The bronc groaned, snorted, inflated its belly, tried to sink down. Savage kicks and lusty curses brought it up. From the announcer's stand came:

"Grey Sage out of chute number one on Widow-Maker!"

The mighty cheer that arose from the crowd was barely audible to the roaring ears of the cowboy who had tossed a leg over the top plank and climbed down inside. Again the bronc fell to beating its head savagely against the chute, trying to pitch. But the close pen and the hostlers thwarted its efforts.

Then Grey was aboard, was shifting his weight about to get the feel of leather. With infinite care he fingered up the single halter-rope, tried it for length. He knew that rope must be right. Too little slack would upset the bronc, too much would bring a breastbone crashing against the horn.

His booted feet found the stirrups, moved forward. Spurred heels poised above the outlaw's shoulders.

With his free hand he jammed down his hat. The trace of a smile moved his lips.

"Let me have him." His voice was quiet, yet it carried a vibrant, high-pitched note.

The flank-strap was jerked up. The chute-gate screeched on rusty hinges. Hostlers leaped to safety. A split second the bronc stood bundled like a cougar. Jangling rowels gouged hair from its taut shoulders. A bellow of rage. It quit the chute like a thunderbolt. One of Grey's legs side-swiped the gate. Sickening pain shot through him. He felt dizzy, nauseated. For an instant he was thrown off balance.

The brute hit the hard-packed ground on legs stiff as pistons. Grey fought desperately to regain his equilibrium, clear the cobwebs of pain from his head. The bronc buried flaring nostrils between hairy fetlocks. The arena became a crazily canting whirl. Grey managed to cling, riding mechanically, scarcely aware of things about him, a part of the half-ton of brawn and hell which, bowed like a hairpin, was lunging away, zig-zagging, sun-fishing, bucking viciously.

The crowd upheaved with a thunderous cheer.

Out of that roar only one voice came clearly to Grey Sage—the voice of a girl.

He tore his gaze from the plastered ears of the bronc to glance about. She was standing near the chutes, beside a big cowboy in goathair chaps. He got a glimpse of her face—a single, fleeting glimpse. On his jumbled consciousness beat one thought: she was the prettiest girl he had ever seen. And there was fear for him in her large brown eyes, in the movement of a hand which flew to her mouth as though to stifle a scream.

Sight of her—momentary as it had been—gave him courage to endure the awful pain in his leg. All his life he had wanted to see such a woman, he was thinking in a hazy, cluttered way. He wondered if she was a Western girl. For old Mason's warning was humming in his ears: "Get a girl of the West . . . one raised to the sage-brush."

But this girl . . . and the big fellow in the goathair chaps alongside of her. It was Barrington—Hugh Barrington, the cowboy he had to defeat to win these finals. Barrington had made a great ride on a bad horse. To beat him meant putting everything he had into the effort.

The terrific punishment he was undergoing drove the girl from his mind. It had whipped every trace of colour from his lean, tanned cheeks. His lips were bloodless, his grey eyes bloodshot, glassy. The furious speed of the outlaw had him gasping. Its bone-crunching lunges threatened to split him in two. He wished his stirrups were a trifle shorter. Then they might break the force of the smashing blows against the saddle. Equilibrium, rhythm, on which he had prided himself aboard a pitching horse, were gone. He was trying desperately to hold his left arm outstretched—not so much now for balance, as to keep the feel of direction, the wildly careening brute now clearing the ground, now heaving over on its side, now struggling for its own footing.

With the instinct of a bronc-rider, he rowelled the outlaw on the shoulders, far back of the cinch. Each time the animal left the ground the arena glided away sickeningly, gave Grey a sinking sensation in the pit of his stomach, increased the nausea that threatened to overwhelm him. Each time it sun-fished, belly up, landed with the force of a pile-driver in front, double-barrelled deadly behind, it rattled his teeth, sent pains shooting through his leg. Damn that leg! He was having trouble finding the frenzied brute beneath him with it.

The first jump had sent his hat sailing. A shock of sandy hair had tumbled into his eyes. The second jump brought blood spurting from his nose. The third . . . he couldn't recall it now. The cantle of the saddle was smashing him with such force as to dull his brain, set shafts of blinding light flashing before his blurred vision.

He was riding for all he was worth; riding gamely, recklessly, pitting the hard muscle of youth against the mountain of untamed horse-flesh. He was putting everything he had in this ride. It was his chance—the chance he had wanted all his life. In the next few jumps he could win or lose a championship. But his leg . . . God, how it hurt! Why should it have happened on this particular ride? It might cost him . . . No, he'd be damned if it would!

Above the drumming of blood in his ears, he caught only snatches of the roar of praise, faintly, far away. Yet, strangely, he seemed always to hear the voice of the girl. And from the corner of his eye he caught occasional glimpses of her as the bronc swapped ends in the arena.

He forced his leg forward to sink bloody rowels into the bay's heaving shoulders. It had been an eternity since he left the chute. That pain was increasing. If only he could drive it from his mind for a few moments longer. The girl . . . she was watching him. Why not make this ride for her? In his young idealism, he longed for a tangible thing he could love, a thing for which he could put forth every effort. True, there was always the memory of his mother. Somehow, it took a woman —such a woman as this girl beside the chute—to fill the emptiness that existed in his life. He would win for her. He would . . .

Damn that leg! It was unnerving him. It felt

now as though it were being pierced through and through with hot irons.

Half-way to the brute's shoulder it stopped, stiff with pain. He struggled to draw it back before the precarious position destroyed his uncertain balance. The effort set his head to reeling. Like a prize-fighter out on his feet, he gave up all attempts to scratch the horse, took to coasting, rowels set, attempting now only to stay. He wondered if she would see it.

That pain was drenching him with cold sweat. Defeat flashed into his mind. The notion brought his spurs to lashing out savagely. All the punishment he had endured in the three days' riding before the cheering thousands at the Arapahoe Stampede suddenly centred in one heart-breaking moment. His leg went useless. For all he could do, his battered body rebelled at further abuse.

Widow-Maker they called the great bay animal he rode—Widow-Maker, the jughead. And jughead it was, its ill-shapen head out of all proportion to its body. It was one of those outlaws that occasionally find their way into the rodeo arenas to blast in a few seconds the championship dreams of years. It lacked the finer instincts of a real horse. It knew only how to maim and trample and kill. The sight of a human being goaded it to fury. Never yet had it bowed to the mastery of man. Six sweating, cursing punchers, with ropes about its rump, had fought to drag it into the chute and saddle it for this ride in the finals. And Grey Sage, his strength taxed to the limit by previous performance, his leg almost shattered by the impact against the gate, had set out to conquer it alone.

For all the seemingly endless hours of torture that had passed since he had catapulted forth aboard the jughead, the ten-second gun had not yet sounded. Stranger still, the outlaw showed no signs of tiring. Perhaps it was because he himself had weakened. But its lunges seemed more savage, its great muscles more like spring steel beneath him.

Hope, ambition faded, driven from a hazy mind by pain. He could endure the torture no longer, no longer could he maintain a knee-grip. He was dimly aware that he was canting far off balance, slapping about crazily in the saddle. He closed his eyes for a second to blot out the sight of the saddle-horn bobbing so invitingly within easy reach. Never in his life had he gone for leather. He wouldn't go for it now. What would his father think, had he known? What would old Mason think . . . old Mason who had faith in him, who had staked him for this very thing? And his mother . . . the girl by the chute?

He caught another glimpse of her as the bronc whirled. She had both hands and her hand-kerchief to her mouth now. She was crying something. He couldn't make out what it was. But there was a strange light in her eyes—a light of encouragement, of hope . . . hope of victory for him.

He put all he had into one last desperate effort. In spite of it the cramped foot of his injured leg began to slide from the stirrup. On his scrambled senses burst the awful realization that for the first time in his life he was doomed to defeat by a horse—defeat by a horse when a championship lay within his reach. Grey Sage, who had taken a boastful pride in telling old Mason that he had never been thrown, that he feared no horse! He didn't and he hadn't—until now. He was slipping. He could stay one more jump—possibly two.

Somewhere out of the infinite whirling space about him roared a gun. A crazy sound burst from his chalk-white lips. The pick-up rider was closing in, reaching for him. He tried to seize the cowboy round the shoulders, let go all holds, hurled himself off blindly. Through a choking cloud of dust the earth flew up to meet him. He landed with an impact that drove the breath from his lungs, sprawled out overwhelmed by a sickening sense of failure—battered, bruised, beaten.

From across a seemingly endless expanse came a voice to throb on his dim consciousness.

"Grey Sage, a Wyoming cowboy, wins the

bronc-riding finals!" It was the announcer bellowing through a megaphone to the excited crowds in the grand-stand. "Grey Sage stayed with Widow-Maker for ten seconds—the first man in rodeo history to do it. Three cheers, ladies and gentleman, for Grey Sage, the new world-champion bronc-rider."

The mighty roar that ascended was but a whisper in Grey's pounding ears. But it brought him up on his elbow. He was stretched in the dirt of the rodeo field. Through suffocating clouds of dust he caught sight of pick-up riders rowelling about trying to haze the still pitching Widow-Maker into the corrals. A doctor, medicine-kit in hand, was coming on a trot. The medico was bending over him, feeling for broken bones. The girl beside the chute . . . his eyes sought for her frantically. She was gone.

Another thunderous cheer. Slowly its meaning dawned on Grey. For all the terrible punishment, for all his seemingly hopeless effort, he had managed to stay with the notorious Widow-Maker for ten seconds.

He lurched to his feet, pushed the doctor aside to stand swaying dizzily, his numb leg buckling under him. He made a bold attempt to appear normal by slapping the dust from his clothes. Time and again he came near falling. He persisted and won. The arena presently stopped its crazy spinning. But the awful burning of a restored circulation in his leg set him to gritting his teeth to keep from crying out. He started limping away towards the chutes, swiping the blood and sweat and grime from his face, tears of agony from his eyes. Half-way, and an angry roar halted him.

"Not by a damned sight Grey Sage isn't the champion," someone was bawling furiously. "Damn him, he was bucked down. My men weren't. You can't pull a whizzer like this on us and get away with it. Widow-Maker's record still stands. Two hundred times out of the chute without a qualified ride on him. This four-flusher's foot was out of the stirrup at the gun. He didn't jump for that pick-up horse. He started leaving the saddle a split second before the gun . . . thrown slick and clean . . . at least dis-qualified. Champion, hell! Don't you wallopers know your own rules?"

"You're a damned liar!" Before Grey was aware of what he was about, he had shaken off his dizziness. In the hot anger of the moment his leg suddenly was forgotten. He was going on a run towards the speaker, who spun about at the sound of his voice.

Chapter IV

Grey Sage halted. His eyes whipped the fellow from head to foot—a beefy man who glistened with silver from the band of a huge hat to big, rowelled, inlaid spurs on the heels of fancy-stitched boots, into which were tucked loud-checked trousers. A cowhide vest with ornate frogs hung loosely about broad shoulders. A conchas-studded belt encircled a bulging paunch. Wind and sun had corrugated his bulldog face. Deep-set eyes, which peered out from beneath shaggy, sun-burned brows, were small and black and cunning. They fastened upon Grey.

"That's big talk for a drifter." The fellow's thick lips curled as he spoke. "Big talk takes backing in this country. You know damned well you were disqualified. Of course, your play is to try to bluff your way through." With a surprisingly agile movement for one of his ponderous bulk, he bounded over to plant himself spread-legged before Grey. "No man riding to-day can scratch that Widow-Maker horse for ten seconds."

"I did," Grey defended, although conscious of a sickening sense of doubt. His gaze darted about in search of the girl he had seen beside the chute. She was nowhere in sight. He was thankful. He did not want her to hear this cheap brawl. Perhaps she had not stayed even long enough to see how near he had come to being thrown. If she had, he hoped she, like the judges, believed he had made his ride. There was more foundation for this fellow's protest than he cared to admit. After all, his foot had been out of the stirrup—on account of the damned leg that even now would barely support his weight. If he had won, it had been by a hairbreadth. Yet there was nothing for him to do but defend it. And he had been on the horse at the ten-second gun.

"I quit that brute after the gun," he heard himself saying. "I've won a thousand bucks at this rodeo. Every cent of it says I can ride Widow-Maker or any other horse you've got, any time, anywhere. You've made your play to the grand-stand, jasper. Now your bluff is called. Money talks."

"Climb back on Widow-Maker right now to prove your ride was qualified, and I'll drop this protest," the big fellow challenged. "I happen to own that horse. He's bucked for three years, and never a cowboy has stuck with him. Have you got the guts to demand a re-ride on Widow-Maker?"

His tone was furious, his beefy body taut. But the fearless manner of Grey Sage warned him to caution. The bulge of the cowboy's lean, clamped jaw sent him back a pace. The determined set of the young-old features—the pleasant features of youth, yet withal the mature face of a man who rushed into danger with reckless disregard of consequences—put a damper on his boiling rage. The battleship-grey eyes, in which there was no fear, were sweeping him arrogantly.

The judges were leaning over the railing of the stand to catch the argument.

"I'm demanding this jasper, who sets himself up as a champion bronc-peeler, be given a re-ride on Widow-Maker."

"And don't think for a minute I won't take it," Grey cried. Damn that leg, it had taken to throbbing again! "Run in all the horses you've got . . . I'll ride 'em. Throw Widow-Maker back into the chute. I'll ride him plumb down—so he'll never pitch again."

"We've got a little something to say about this." It was the announcer, after a hurried conference with the judges. "You made your ride, Sage . . . one of the best we ever saw in Arapahoe. It satisfied the judges, and we're betting it satisfied everybody else."

Those of the crowd able to edge in close enough to hear yelled their approval.

"If you feel you have a complaint coming, we're willing to give you better than an even break. You mentioned that none of your men were bucked down. We'll do this: If there is a one of them wants to climb aboard Widow-Maker and will stick for ten seconds, like Grey Sage did, we'll reconsider our decision and give them both a re-ride."

A moment of portentous calm. The crowd stringing out of the grand-stand shoved and pushed to get nearer, only to wedge into a hopelessly packed mass. Grey Sage stood scarcely moving—all but his eyes. Again they were searching futilely for the girl. The big fellow's eyes were riveted upon a group of cowboys near the chutes, saddling their horses.

"There isn't a one of your men want any of Widow-Maker," the announcer taunted. "Yet Grey Sage didn't shy away from the brute when he drew him. Sage has come out on the worst buckers every day of the show. Well, what do you say? We're still waiting to hear from your buckaroos."

The crowd wedged in tighter—a great, swaying, weaving mass that was pushing the front line close about the two men in the arena. Every eye now was upon the cowboys at the chutes. But if the punchers so much as heard, they gave no indication—they only went about their saddling.

"Barrington!" the big fellow boomed. "You're second-money man. Will you force this jasper to a re-ride by coming out on Widow-Maker?"

Hugh Barrington, a heavily built cowboy of wind-whipped face and blue eyes—cold, with the suggestion of burnished steel in their depths—

straightened up to stand with thumbs hooked in the belt of his goathair chaps. A handsome devil, Grey thought as he recognized him—and a hard-riding cowboy of championship calibre. It had been Barrington who stood beside the pretty girl while he was making his ride on Widow-Maker. But the girl was with him no longer.

"Hell, no!" the cowboy was speaking, in a deep voice that carried across the arena. "That jasper earned everything he won on that jughead. What difference does it make if his foot was out of the stirrup at the gun? He rode the hellion, didn't he? Me, I'm not caring to try to steal his laurels by letting that outlaw kink my neck."

The reply brought thunderous cheers from the crowd, set the big fellow to cursing.

"What's the matter, Barrington?" he yelled. "Scared . . . showing yellow?"

Angry flame laced the cowboy's eyes.

"You've known me for quite a spell, Harmon," Grey Sage made mental note of the name. "Did you ever know me to show yellow on a horse—or anywhere else?" There was a cold fearlessness, a challenge in Barrington's tone.

"I didn't mean that," Harmon offered apologetically.

"Then say what you mean." Barrington tried his saddle by the horn, swung on to his horse. Reining about, he rode directly to Grey Sage. Beside the cowboy he stopped, leaned over, extended his hand. Grey took it—the clasp of two strong men who looked deep into one another's eyes, plumbed the depths of each other's souls.

"You made a great ride, jasper," Barrington said, with a ring of sincerity in his voice. "I'm satisfied to take second money because I can't ride Widow-Maker. As for this ring-tailed rannyhan"—he jerked a thumb at the boiling Harmon—"he'd just have so much belly-ache coming no matter what happened." He shifted sidewise in the saddle to face Harmon. "Now I'll either go back to the ranch as your foreman or go on from here. Suit yourself. I don't care a damn one way or another."

"Forget it . . . forget it, Barrington," Harmon sputtered. "Just one of those things that come up. Don't get on your high horse."

Barrington lifted his mount with the rowels, threw dust into the open mouth of the apoplectic Harmon, who whirled back on Grey. But before he could speak the announcer shouted:

"The judges are declaring Grey Sage the champion bronc-rider—"

"Then another year you'll pull your show without my stock," Harmon roared. "Widow-Maker is the greatest drawing-card you'll ever have—a horse that's never been ridden. I'm protesting, I tell you. I'll go clean over your heads to the National Association."

"That being the case, folks," the announcer

said, to be rid of the uneasy crowd, "we have no alternative but to submit our charts to the Association. Until we have an official ruling on this contest we cannot declare Grey Sage the winner. We're sorry, but . . . Arapahoe is bidding you all so-long . . . and telling you that we'll be at the same old stand next year."

"You'll hear more about this," the big fellow hurled at Grey. "You can't make fools of the Cross Anchor and get away with it. Hugh Barrington can give you cards and spades and buck you down any day if he just has a mind to. As long as he won't, I'm protesting your ride. And I'm calling that thousand-dollar bet you made—calling your bluff that you can ride any horse I've got any time, anywhere and scratch him."

"I'm snorting to go," Grey shot back.

"All right, then be sure you don't lose your guts and take a *pasear* out of the country. Have that thousand handy. Because I'm collecting it. Before the Cross Anchor gets through with you, you'll wish you'd have stayed with your sheep."

A blazing retort formed on Grey's grimly pursed lips. But he had no chance to give it utterance. The big fellow spun about, was quickly swallowed up in the crowd.

Grey, too, turned to the corrals to secure his horse. The announcer, in the stand above, halted him.

"We always have a little dinner for our top riders," he said good-naturedly. "We present our prizes there. At the Ashmore Hotel. Seven-thirty to-night. The cowboys will all be there . . . and the rodeo committee. You'll come?"

In the sudden panic that assailed him, Grey Sage was on the point of refusing. In his present mood he wanted to be alone. For all his valiant effort, his ride had been protested. He had failed, fallen just short of the coveted goal—as he always seemed to fall short of successful achievement. He had failed because of that damned leg. In his heart he knew he hadn't won the contest. His foot had been out of the stirrup. Another time, though, he'd show them: show them that the dreams of becoming a champion rider could materialize. But a dinner at a big hotel—that was something different.

"Sure thing, and much obliged," he found himself saying as he passed on towards the corrals—hastily, to cover his embarrassment.

Chapter V

By now the crowd had spread out in a great human fan over the arena to converge on the exits and creep from the grounds. Oldsters managed to move forward but a step at a time in the tight-packed mass. Children darted in and out with apparent ease, frantic parents shouting, attempting without success to keep track of restless broods.

Near the chutes Grey Sage paused to watch that slow-moving throng, the largest he ever had seen. At the moment the homestead back in the arid reaches of the Cheyenne River—where an occasional passing rider was an event—seemed far, far away, as though he had known it and its vast solitude only in hazy memory. He had been lonely to the point of madness there. The days without sight of a human being had seemed interminable. Yet now, strangely, with all these thousands about him, he suddenly was lonelier than ever.

"What the hell do you want?" He mentally berated himself for the contradictory emotions that surged up within him. "When you are alone, you want crowds. When you are in crowds, you want to be alone. You can't have everything. You've got to be satisfied with something." Yet, for all he could do, there still remained the hollow gnawing of loneliness deep within him.

The honours he had won? While they elated him to a degree, they were not what he had anticipated. Somehow the adulation of the thrill-seeking thousands seemed empty and unreal. Success, he found suddenly, was not, as he had always believed, a thing attained simply through the plaudits of a hero-worshipping throng. Success was something far deeper—something within oneself, even though it drew neither cheer nor tear.

Anticipation . . . dreams? For the first time he realized they were far pleasanter than reality, although he was forced to admit a certain pride within him at achievement that drew applause. His battle with Widow-Maker—known the world over as the unridable horse—had drawn the cheers of the fickle throng. Within a week, apart from an occasional remark, they would probably have forgotten his struggle. Desperate it had been. And it had availed him nothing. The championship was still a mythical something just beyond his reach. His attempt to master Widow-Maker had fallen far short of champion performance. Harmon knew, and he knew, that he had not bucked the outlaw down. That injured leg had snatched from him complete victory.

He tried to tell himself he had won some sort of success—at least honour and cheers. If only

Mason were here to share it with him! That was what he wanted. Not so much fame and glory, but companionship—close, understanding companionship. He never had known it, apart from Mason. But, young as he was, he knew that old age never could meet youth on its own ground—for old age lives in the past; youth's dreams are always of the future.

He found himself searching the crowd for a glimpse of somebody he knew—a glimpse of that girl who had been with the cowboy, Barrington. Fine fellow, Barrington. A man he would like to know better. But the girl. Was she his sister? They hadn't seemed like man and wife. They were too poorly matched for that. He was big, broad-shouldered, masterful—a man's man. She was slender, dainty, not exactly delicate. As he recalled her, she was strong-looking in her smallness, delicate only in the way of a gumbo-lily on the prairies, surviving in an arid land where other vegetation withered and died. He couldn't bring himself to believe there was a marital relationship between these two.

He turned again towards the corrals. Save for a slight soreness, his leg no longer hurt him. He had forgotten it completely in the excitement. Strange, he thought, how pain that dominated one, perhaps changed the course of a life, suddenly vanished into nothingness when driven from mind.

Damn that dinner! He wished it wasn't necessary. Of course, there were the prizes . . . he had won a silver-mounted saddle worth five hundred dollars. He thrilled to that. He'd get that, even if Harmon's protest stood. He had admired it the night before in the window of a harness-shop. There were also cash awards—a thousand dollars at least. And a trophy that would be his if he really had won it and could win it two more times. A shower of honours for which he had never dared hope. Yet he dreaded appearing at that dinner to claim them—dreaded it more than he had his first walk across the arena towards the chutes under the eyes of watching thousands.

He had never been at a dinner where people came for any other purpose than to eat. His table etiquette had been limited to that found on the hard earth during the round-up, the oilcloth-covered tables in the heart of Cowland. There, if people ever had had manners, they had long since forgotten them. He recalled one time when the boys at the ranch had been invited to dine with a cowboy who had just married an Eastern schoolteacher. Dinner had been served in a sheepwagon—a dinner of white linen, beautiful silverware and pitifully little food. He remembered how embarrassed the cowhands had been, watching each other to see what they would do with the knives and forks. Once through the ordeal, they had ridden back to the mess-wagon to rout out the cook and make him prepare them some food.

This dinner, though, was one of those distasteful yet unavoidable things, he realized, that would come regularly out here in this world of people. Much as he dreaded it, he must attend.

A sudden thought threw him into a new panic. He had no clothes. He could scarcely appear in the overalls, chaps and high-heeled boots that constituted his present garb. His hand went to his pocket. He pulled forth the few tight-rolled bills. Twenty dollars! Enough, perhaps, to buy a cheap suit. He would have more to-night, when the rodeo committee paid him—more money than he had ever seen at one time. Yes, he would buy himself a suit . . . doll up. The resolve momentarily buoyed his spirits.

He stepped aside for a band of saddle-horses, driven by cowboys. About him now the hostlers were releasing the wild stock—great Brahma steers, with a hump on their shoulders, that were thrown into a herd to be run to the railroad yards or to neighbouring ranches. Wiry calves that had eluded the crack ropers. Roping-horses, saddled, with breast-strap or martingale—dainty-stepping little fellows that minced along, necks arched proudly—hulking bulls that tossed their heads, snorted, stopped to paw the earth belligerently. The stock moved past in a cloud of dust. The crowd was thinning at the exits.

With a sigh at having come finally to the end of a great adventure, Grey turned again towards the corrals. He had taken no more than half a dozen steps when a shout halted him. He spun about, startled. One of the bulls had broken from the herd, started madly across the arena.

A girl also had whirled on the rear edge of the crowd. People bolted away from her. For an instant she stood motionless. Apparently realizing she was alone, she, too, started to run. Not, however, in the direction of the exit. In sudden panic she set off down the field towards a lower gate. She was garbed in red. The bull let forth a thunderous bellow, downed its great head and charged after her.

Attempting to hold the rest of the stock, which in the confusion was trying to break in all directions, seconds ticked off before the cowboys were even aware of the girl's plight.

By now a crescendoing cry of warning had arisen from the crowd which had stopped, frozen in its tracks. Of all the watching hundreds, Grey Sage alone acted. In a dozen bounds he had gained the bunch of saddled roping-horses. He vaulted up over the rump of a bay, landed in the saddle. He jerked the halter-rope from a cowboy's hand, lifted the animal in a gravel-flinging lunge down the field. Rowels raked tufts of hair from sleek and heaving sides. The brute fled like a frightened deer.

Despite the suddenness with which he had made his choice, Grey had picked well his mount. The horse quickly cut in half the distance that separated it from the lumbering, bellowing bull.

The girl in red ran on, breathlessly now. And she was losing ground in the mad race with the charging animal. She stopped, started to turn back towards the crowd. Sight of the savage oncoming brute terrified her out of her senses. She raced on.

But her movements lacked speed. She was giving out swiftly. The glimpse Grey Sage caught of her chalk-white face sent his spurs deeper into the horse.

Then, of a sudden, his heart seemed to miss a beat. The girl had stumbled. A scant hundred yards now separated her from the charging bull. He rowelled savagely. The horse was doing its utmost.

Strong momentarily with a strength born of fear, the girl struggled to her feet, was running again. The bull, too, had veered off after the red dress that infuriated him, and had given Grey a slight advantage equal to two or three of the swiftly moving horse's leaps.

Now the little bay was pulling alongside the animal. Its lunges kept the saddle buckling on its humping back. Above the roar of the wind in his ears Grey could hear the girl's stifled sobs, hear the cowboys now thundering along behind them, hear the whistle of looped ropes slicing the air. But at the pace his pony was setting none but himself could hope to reach her in time—if indeed he could.

Not more than fifty yards now separated the charging brute from its terrified quarry. It let forth a rumbling bawl of victory, seemed to bundle itself into greater leaps towards the moving red dress.

Grey lifted his horse alongside, was neck and neck with the animal. He pulled rein, fearful that, at the breakneck speed, he himself might run down the girl. Knotting the bridle-reins, he dropped them across the horn, freed one foot from the stirrup. He leaned far over in the saddle. Accustomed to any manner of riding, the horse hugged the bull's side. Grey let go all holds, shot off into space. Once free of his weight, the horse wheeled. The girl, on the verge of collapse, was reeling wearily.

Grey landed between the lowered horns of the bull. A great cloud of dust arose. Grey's heels dug into the ground, slackened the pace of the infuriated brute. Down went its horns under his weight. One ploughed into the earth, shattered with a sickening crunch. The bull went end-over-end. The girl, too, had fallen. Neither rose. The bull shuddered, stretched out, its neck doubled back beneath its body.

Grey leaped to his feet, sprang over to the prostrate girl. The cowboys thundered up.

"Nice work," one lauded. "Pretty a job of bull-dogging as we've seen. But pegging disqualifies you."

"What would you have done?" Grey grinned up at him.

"I couldn't have thought that fast," was the frank admission. "I'd probably have let the bull win the race. But you'll get hell for it."

"Why?"

"It's one of Harmon's crack bulls." The cowboy leaped from his horse. By now the crowd was pouring back into the arena. Grey picked up the girl in his arms, started towards the main exit.

For the first time, he had a good look at her. That look brought colour to his face. Afterwards he recalled the sensation. It was as though something had struck him a violent blow. Never before had he seen such a pretty girl—far prettier than the girl who had watched him make his ride—and different. How? He did not know. All he knew at the moment was that he held in his arms a girl whose beauty thrilled him. A sudden panic assailed him. She might be injured. Perhaps she was dead. But he knew she wasn't. He could feel her breathing. Yet the terrifying notion persisted.

Her body was firm and strong in his arms, shapely from the tips of her daintily-clad feet to the jet-black hair now sadly disarrayed on her head. The wind whipped the red silken dress up round alluring ankles to reveal tapering legs sheathed in the sheerest of hosiery.

Conscious of an increasing embarrassment as he neared the crowd, Grey would have put her down. But fear for her safety kept him moving along awkwardly.

Into her pale, agate-smooth face was coming a tinge. Once he thought the long lashes that lay over her closed eyes were fluttering. And the ears that peeked from beneath her mass of black hair were coral-tinted like the drops in her earrings.

"You danged fool," was the sobering mental reaction he voiced to himself. "She's just a girl."

"But a blamed pretty one," he found some inner voice assuring him. "And when she opens her eyes they'll be black—big and black and lustrous to match her hair."

Then he was in the crowd with his alluring burden. From somewhere came an improvised stretcher. Grey lowered the girl tenderly.

He gulped, blinked, tried to pull away. Shapely white arms were about his neck, she was clinging to him frantically, fearfully.

"Save me," she choked. "That . . ." Her eyes fluttered open. Something of elation surged through Grey. As he expected, they were black—jet black as her hair—and sincere, for all the fear that now flared in their limpid depths.

She regarded him for a moment in wide-eyed

surprise—a surprise that struck Grey as strange. Then the arms about his neck relaxed. But instead of falling back on the stretcher, she struggled to her feet.

"Oh," she said in a low voice, a voice huskily musical, "I'm . . ." Her frightened glance swept the crowd. "I want to thank you . . . but it's too public here." She started away dizzily, clinging to his hand.

For an instant he hung back, terribly embarrassed. Later he regretted it. The crowd surged in. The girl was torn from him. A tremendous shout went up. For all his struggle, Grey was hoisted on the shoulders of brawny punchers to be carried about the arena, his face blazing as he tried futilely to free himself. His eyes searched the crowd for the girl. She was gone—gone without giving him a chance to find out her name. He cursed himself for all kinds of an idiot. But there was nothing he could do at the moment—until these fools released him.

"Prettiest job of hoolihaning ever seen in these parts," he heard two grizzled cowmen shouting at each other as they bore him along. "But Harmon is going to raise particular hell. That was his prize bull."

Grey freed himself. Leaping down, he ducked away, from the cheers of the crowd. He scarcely heard them. He was searching for the girl in red.

A sudden thought halted him. It was getting late. Already the sun had set. A murky haze of dust hung low over the shadowed field. He must hurry, or the stores would be closed. He trotted back to secure his horse. It nickered in a friendly fashion as he came up, as though it too were lonely in the mass of animals and humans.

Then he was in the saddle, had whirled and was rowelling away towards town, searching every group for a glimpse of the girl in red, or a glimpse of the girl who had been the companion of Hugh Barrington at the chutes during his ride. It did not make a great deal of difference which one he saw, he admitted to himself—just so he saw one of them.

Chapter VI

With far less assurance than when climbing the chutes at the rodeo-grounds under the eyes of watching thousands Grey Sage made his way into the lobby of the big Ashmore hotel that evening, dreadfully uncomfortable in the store clothes he had purchased with the last of the money old Mason had loaned him: a plain blue serge suit, which, fortunately, fitted him as though it had been tailored, a high white collar that choked him, a black four-in-hand tie and new shoes that hurt his feet.

He prowled about trying to appear at ease. His efforts to hide his embarrassment only made it more noticeable. He felt too big for his clothes, too awkward for the close confinement. Once as he strolled he got a glimpse of himself in a glass. The image startled him. His tanned face above the white collar reminded him of an Indian.

"Mr. Grey Sage?"

A pretty girl in smart uniform, with jaunty red cap cocked on the side of her head, touched his arm.

"Yes."

The cowboy whirled nervously, ashamed of his uneasiness, but powerless to overcome it.

"The Chamber of Commerce dinner is in the main dining-room. I was told to bring you there. Follow me, please."

Conscious of the stares of every one about the lobby, aware that conversation had ceased, he strode along after the girl. Came to him a flash of wonder that he was even managing to walk straight, so great was his embarrassment.

Then they were at the door of the dining-room. The girl took his hat. He surrendered it without protest, although the thought did come to him how he ever would find it again. With a last hitch at his plain black tie—knotted neatly, thanks to the storekeeper—and smoothing down his coat, he stepped into the room.

Before him was spread a great table. Faces ran in seemingly endless rows along its sides—faces blurred to his quick-shifting eyes, which, in his nervousness, attempted to include everything in a single glance. His survey of the group ended as suddenly as the buzz of conversation that left things deathly still except for his pounding ears. Came to him a wild thought to flee while there was yet time. He steeled himself to the ordeal, stood staring before the friendly nods that greeted him—staring in a sickly way that left the smile frozen on his thin lips.

He knew he should do something. But what? To his amazement, he was bowing. The longer he stood, singled out as a target for every gaze, the more panicky he became. Next morning he recalled, with a sort of lazy pride, that it really hadn't been so bad after all, that entrance into the banquet-room. But now . . .

It was the announcer from the rodeo-field who had risen from the table and was coming forward, hand outstretched.

"Glad to see you, Sage," he was saying in a way that mitigated Grey's embarrassment, would have put him at some sort of ease but for another discovery—a discovery that increased the urge to flee. He had expected only men. There were women at the table. His grey eyes darted among them, but still those faces ran together in jagged lines. His knees felt like tallow, had taken to shaking so violently they threatened to give way under his weight.

"Ladies and gentlemen . . ." The announcer was addressing the diners. ". . . I have the pleasure of introducing to you as a group at this time, individually later, I hope—Grey Sage, one of the finest riders ever presented at the stampede and who, but for an unfortunate incident, would have been crowned world champion to-day."

The diners came to their feet with a cheer. Men and women were bowing. Now Grey was positive he couldn't go through with the thing. He wanted to hide, be alone, if only for a moment, to brace himself, get hold of his jumpy nerves. Now the homestead in the far reaches of the Cheyenne River range-country seemed like a paradise of peace and solitude.

But he had little time to think. The announcer, whom he knew as Tommy Brown, was leading him forward. He was walking stiff-legged to keep his knees from buckling. His heels were clacking loudly.

A white-clad waiter pulled back a chair at the head of the table. Striving desperately to display some semblance of ease, Grey started to sit down while the attendant waited. He straightened up again, shoulders squared. He blinked, gulped, muttered something—he was not quite sure what. For directly on his left sat the girl, the pretty girl who had smiled at him and watched him ride from beside the chutes. She was looking up at him in a way that gave him confidence. His heart went out to her. In her, he knew at a glance, he had found a friend.

But the introduction that followed left him bewildered, conscious of a sense of disappointment.

"This is Mrs. Hugh Barrington," Brown was saying into his ears, that had suddenly started to roar.

Then the girl had offered him her hand—a friendly, typically Western gesture. He took it, scarcely knowing what he did, although he could not suppress the thrill that little hand gave him as it lay in his. Her proffer of friendship, plainly designed to put him at his ease, made him certain of one thing—she was a girl of the West who recognized and understood his embarrassment, who knew the mental agony he was enduring.

Then he was shaking hands again with her husband—Barrington, the cowboy who had refused to force him into a re-ride. The puncher's clasp was strong. There was something big and unselfish in this Barrington that won him instantly.

"And this is Miss Alice Harmon," Brown was saying.

Grey's heart took to pounding savagely. The contraction of his dry throat was cutting off his breath. On his right sat the girl of the red dress he had saved from the infuriated bull.

"And from what we hear . . ." Brown seemed to be shouting into his ears, ringing with the infernal din of pulsing blood. ". . . Miss Harmon has you to thank that she is here to-night."

Grey's eyes met those of the girl. Again he looked into the depths of the black orbs that had stirred him so strangely when he had held her in his arms back at the rodeo-grounds. Something passed between them: some unexplainable thing that for the moment left them both speechless. This girl, too, had offered her hand. It lay in his palm languidly. He made a quick mental com-parison of the way Mrs. Barrington's hand had felt.

"Thank you," the girl was murmuring, although

her eyes had fallen before the gaze he seemed unable to control, the gaze he knew was regarding her too steadily for comfort. "I did not get a chance at the grounds. It was very brave . . . and fine."

"It was nothing." He scarcely recognized his own tone.

"It was something," the man beside the girl boomed out in a voice that startled Grey, brought his eyes flashing up. It was the fellow who had protested his ride aboard Widow-Maker.

"I'm John Harmon—Colonel John Harmon—and I, too, am thanking you."

Alice Harmon . . . Colonel John Harmon. The names suddenly ran together in Grey's brain. Was this lovely girl he had rescued the wife of this big man? Surely not. But the other woman? She was the wife of Barrington. A momentary sickening doubt assailed him. Yet Brown had called her Miss.

Brown was talking now.

"Miss Harmon is here from the East . . . visiting this summer with her uncle, Colonel Harmon. Colonel Harmon furnishes the wild stock for our show . . . owns a big dude ranch out in the Casper mountains. And . . . he also owns a horse named Widow-Maker."

A flush darkened Harmon's bulldog features.

"A horse that has never been qualified on at any rodeo," he blurted out. "I'm still holding it against your committee, Brown. No offence, Sage," he offered quickly to Grey, "but that horse has hung up a world record. He has pitched from England to Australia and always got his man. Maybe you can understand now why I was so r'iled up about it. I regret the incident, but—"

"That's all right." Grey smiled, more at ease now that he was face to face with the man under different circumstances. But, he noticed, Harmon did not look him in the eye, nor did his words ring true.

Grey finally managed to sit down and tried desperately to regain his composure. For a moment he had ceased to be the centre of attraction, for which he was thankful. The girl, Alice Harmon, was smiling at him. And now he had time to study her with furtive glances. She was dressed in a daringly low-cut gown of black that matched her eyes, brought out the gleaming quality of her raven-black hair. Somehow she reminded him of a princess. Yet there was something about her that chilled him and made him a little fearful. Perhaps it was her confidence, the graciousness of her talk, which at times he could not but feel was a trifle patronizing.

He made a poor attempt to laugh off the incident at the rodeo-grounds, fell to explaining to her steer bull-dogging or wrestling, with its attendant practices of pegging and hoolihaning. Then they fell silent.

"And you, Mrs. Barrington," he found himself saying with an ease that dumbfounded him as he turned to the smaller woman on his left. "Did you enjoy the rodeo?"

He blinked as their eyes met. Here was a woman who could offer nothing but contrast to Alice Harmon. For where the other's hair was black, this shapely head beside him was crowned with ringlets of brown, brown with a reddish tinge that made it gleam in the shaded light. Where the other's eyes were black, these were brown, large, sincere, incapable, in their frankness, of concealing any emotion. These eyes reminded him of the liquid eyes of a doe. And they held a strange light—a light he could not fathom, but which made him confident, where the other girl's gaze made him ill at ease.

The full red lips of this woman were without rouge, which was just a trifle too thick on the lips of Alice. These lips were arched prettily across shining teeth. For all his attempts not to stare, he could not control his eyes, the eyes of youth that revelled in alluring womanhood. She was gowned in a dainty frock without the low cut that revealed Alice's gleaming white shoulders. And where Alice Harmon wore a string of pearls, this girl beside him was without ornament of any kind. And, he told himself, she needed none. Her beauty was far deeper than her pretty face. She radiated beauty, friendship, sincerity.

After the first contact of gazes—a long while to his nervous senses, but in reality a fleeting glance —she fell to talking in a companionable, comfortable way. With an impulsiveness that set him to tingling, she leaned close and laid a hand on his arm, so close he caught the faint odour of her, sweet and warm.

"How did I like the rodeo?" she asked in a low, bantering tone. "For convention's sake I'd say I enjoyed it immensely, Mr. Sage. But between you and me I'd say it was the cat's pyjamas, cowboy." She threw back her head and laughed, a tingling, musical laugh. His heart was doing strange things. He was trembling under the contact of her fingers which remained on his arm—caressingly, he could have sworn. But she didn't seem like the forward type. No, it was just his imagination. Yet, somehow, they had a common bond. What that bond was he made no attempt to know. He was only conscious at the moment of a stab of regret that this pretty woman was married.

Then her husband was leaning over, talking—the big cowboy who had refused to ride Widow-Maker.

"Remember the first time I went through all this tommy-rot, Judy?" he was asking. "He's probably suffering as much as I did."

"I'll say I am," Grey admitted, feeling that here, at least, were two who understood. "This danged collar is choking me. Seems like I've been poured into these clothes. How long does the thing last?"

Great folks, these Barringtons. It seemed as though he had known them all his life. No use trying to make them believe he was easy in these surroundings. They knew differently.

"Let down, cowboy." The woman, Judy, was speaking again. How the name seemed to fit her. Judy . . . It was almost as pretty as her face. "You look like you're seeing ghosts."

"I am," he blurted out, catching her gaze and holding it in spite of her attempt to lower it.

"I know," she said in a low tone he knew was meant for his ears alone. "I saw them too, back at the chutes to-day."

"You were trying not to scream . . . when I was up on Widow-Maker?" He spoke before he thought.

"Yes." She fell silent.

Barrington started to talk to him, about riding, about the merits of various notorious buckers. And the other girl, Alice, who still terrified him with her cold exterior and graciousness, was talking to him. He tried to answer them both. He got everything all jumbled up.

"I guess everybody would like to have a little speech from a great rider." It was Brown shouting to make himself heard. "Ladies and gentlemen . . . Grey Sage!"

Chapter VII

Grey Sage looked about wildly. He saw faces he had never seen before—countless faces that became an endless sea stretching on and on even beyond the walls of the room. His parched lips went even drier. He touched them with his tongue. Every eye in the room was upon him. He could feel them, though he could not see them. His knees were shaking. He felt a sickish sensation in the pit of his stomach. His first impulse was to slump down, disappear beneath the table.

Make a speech! It was utterly ridiculous . . . at the same time deadly serious. Out of the stark terror of the moment came to him a flash of what old Mason would think.

He dared a glance at Alice. Her expression was set, immobile. No sympathy there. Even the slight smile she essayed made him colder, more fearful, as though she were measuring him, expecting him to fail. Damn her! He'd show her.

Again a little hand was on his arm. His eyes turned to meet those of Judy Barrington.

"Up and at 'em, cowboy," she was encouraging. "Any man who has the nerve to step across Widow-Maker doesn't need to be afraid of this bunch of food-mauling rannyhans. Get yourself a name as a dinner speaker. It might come in handy sometime . . . night-herding."

The hand was actually forcing him to his feet. He shot a glance at Barrington, half expecting him to take exception to the all-too-obvious movement of his wife. But Barrington, fortunately, was looking away.

Grey Sage was on his feet, braced against the table to steady his trembling legs. Once he thought he would take a drink of water. But his hand was shaking too badly, he knew he never could get it to his mouth. The pounding blood in his temples was making his head shake.

"Thank you, ladies and gentlemen," he found himself saying in a strange, high-pitched voice. "I never made a speech before . . . but here goes."

He blinked, stared with unbelieving eyes. Applause had greeted his words. Then again it was quiet—so damnably quiet it reminded him of the flats back on the Cheyenne River. There he had longed for noise and crowds, perhaps applause. Now he had those things and he was terrified, wished frantically for the quiet solitude of the prairies he had tried to make himself believe he hated.

Vaguely aware of the increasing embarrassment due to his own silence, but seemingly unable to prevent it, he risked another glance at Alice. After all, of this whole crowd, she was the only one he really feared. She was looking at him with an intentness that made him feel she was weighing him according to her own standards and finding him woefully lacking. The little hand of Judy Barrington on his left was still patting his fingers that gripped the edge of the table until his knuckles stood out white, bloodless.

"Guess all I can talk about is bronc-riding," he was saying, thickly now, but with more assurance in his wavering tone. "And when you come right down to it, I don't know a lot about that."

"You might tell us how to ride them," Brown suggested in a friendly tone. "Men who climb aboard horses like Widow-Maker know something about it."

"I'll say they do," Barrington put in. "Widow-Maker has thrown me three times in three years. I refused to ride the devil this year, Sage."

"Widow-Maker is a tough horse. The worst I ever rode." Grey shot a glance at Harmon. The big fellow had bellied out importantly, was sweeping the crowd with an air of exaggerated importance.

"I knew it . . . your foot . . ."

"Wasn't out of the stirrup at the pick-up gun," Grey flung in a tone that silenced further argument. "But as I came out of the chute, Widow-Maker lurched against the gate-post. That leg was numb from the second the bronc made the first jump."

"He was hurt," was the whispered comment that ran round the table.

"That's what I told you there by the chutes," Judy was saying to Barrington. "I knew that leg was paining him, that he wasn't scratching the horse like he had the others."

"Nobody does." Grey caught Barrington's reply. "But he was kicking the devil just plenty high, at that—higher than I ever tried to kick him."

"But not enjoying it." Grey smiled—the smile that persisted in freezing on his face. For the life of him he couldn't get it off. It was set, controlled by muscles that felt as loggy and numb as those of his injured leg during the ride. He could almost imagine how silly that grin must look. "I've been riding since I was knee-high to a grasshopper. Never knew anything else. Widow-Maker was the only horse I ever rode that I figured I wouldn't be on top of when the fight was over."

Colonel Harmon led the applause. Grey noticed and wondered. But Alice . . . her face had not moved a muscle. Frozen Face, he called her mentally, for all her beauty. She was watching him so closely it embarrassed him.

"That horse hit me with the cantle-board so hard I saw stars even after I was down." Started,

Grey was rushing on . . . anything to get through. "And my leg . . . but you folks don't want to hear that."

"We do," came a chorus of shouts.

But Grey's shyness had returned. He was becoming speechless; words seemed to refuse to issue from his lips. His tongue was cleaving to the roof of his dry mouth.

"Don't quit, cowboy," came Judy's low voice that only he could hear. "You're knocking them for a whole row of sod-roofed barns. They love it, and . . ." He sent her a swift, inscrutable glance as she paused. ". . . and so do I," she managed to get out before her eyes fell.

It seemed to bolster up his waning nerve.

"Being a bronc-rider, I say, I don't know how to talk. But treat horses like you do folks. They've got plenty of savvy. When you get to know them as they know you, you've made a friend. Take them easy. Don't heave a saddle at them. Barrington"—he met the big cowboy's gaze—"will back me up that mean horses are a heap rarer than mean men."

"You're danged right," the cowboy said. "I've been trying to tell Harmon—"

"Folks go at riding wrong. A cowboy takes it easy. He knows he has to ride his bronc. It's part of his day's work. And he can't feel any fear of the animal. Because once he fears a horse he is through." Hand-clapping checked Grey.

70

"Tell us how to ride broncs," Brown, obviously enjoying the talk, challenged, to Grey's surprise.

"Well, get yourself a horse—the type of Widow-Maker," Grey grinned, looked straight at Harmon, who flushed but managed an icy smile. "Climb into the saddle, easy. Get your halter-rope right, because you can crack up against the horn if it is too short. Stick your rowels up towards the brute's shoulders—not set, for that's against the rules; but hard enough to give you balance. After the bronc makes the first jump and you're sure he's going ahead instead of over backwards, you get direction. From then on everything is easy. All you have to do is to sit up there and teeter. When the bronc goes down, you go back. When the bronc goes up, you go forward, exactly like in a rocking-chair."

"But if he sun-fishes?" Barrington put in. "What do you do then, if it's so danged easy?" Barrington was laughing at him. The crowd now was laughing, but in a way that no longer embarrassed him.

"I'll be danged if I know," Grey admitted. "You've stepped across a good many, Barrington. What do you do to keep your balance when a bronc sun-fishes or swaps ends?"

"I've been trying to tell them right here at this table every stampede banquet for five years." The big cowboy threw back his head and roared. "I came about as close to it as you have. You've made a good stab, Sage. But I reckon you're a wash-out at explaining, too. Some day we're going to find a cowboy who will be able to reveal the secret so everybody can be a top bronc-rider."

"I can show anybody how to ride a bucking horse," Grey blurted out, "but—"

Colonel Harmon got to his feet.

"While I know Mr. Sage has the floor and you want to hear him, I'd like to say right here that if he actually can teach novices to ride either bucking horses or gentle saddle-horses, he's got a job with the Cross Anchor dude ranch."

"And as foreman of your spread I don't know anybody I'd rather have wrangling the guests," Barrington put in, still chuckling. "At least we know he won't put any of them up on horses like Widow-Maker. Want the job, Sage . . . starting to-morrow?"

Grey glanced from one to the other. Then his eyes flew to Alice. Her expression had changed. The frozen critical mask had dropped. Her rich black eyes were pleading. He glanced at Judy Barrington. She lowered her gaze.

"Thanks, Colonel Harmon," he said. "I'd be proud to take the job with your spread. But I'm aiming on making the rounds of the rodeos. I want to go to Pendleton . . . mebbeso east to New York and . . ."

"I'm not overlooking any bets on the publicity

you'll give us riding for the Cross Anchor," Harmon put in quickly. "Is that all that stands in the way?"

"I guess so." Grey berated himself for his easy acquiescence.

"Then, folks, let me introduce Grey Sage to you again. Grey Sage, crack bronc-rider and the new top wrangler of the Cross Anchor dude ranch!"

A cheer went up. Thankful at being out of the spotlight, Grey sat down. Alice leaned over. She placed a hand on his arm, a marble-white hand, glittering with jewels.

"You were wonderful," she whispered.

"Wonderful?" in amazement.

"You were positively rotten," Judy whispered fiercely from the other side. "And I had such hopes for you." He turned swiftly, captured her gaze. A current of emotion surged through him. He stared, bewildered. The glances of the two girls had met. What passed between them Grey Sage never knew. But there was a sudden-sparkle of tears in Judy's eyes. And Alice now was deliberately clasping his hand, that looked brown and awkward beneath her smooth white fingers. If there had been an outlet for flight, Grey now would have taken it.

Chapter VIII

With a mingled sense of elation and utter strangeness, Grey Sage rolled out in the dew-damp dawn the following day. He pulled on his chaps and boots, and stepped outside the bunkhouse.

A smile moved his thin lips. For the bunkhouse that had been turned over to him was far better than any house in which he had ever set foot. As top wrangler for the exclusive Cross Anchor dude ranch, he must have a place befitting his station, Colonel Harmon had explained. And his salary—it was a salary now, not just wages—was fifty dollars a week—more than he had received for a month of hard labour back at the ranches along the Cheyenne River.

He stretched comfortably. Within him stirred a feeling of lazy contentment, a dormant happiness of which he did not think himself capable. It seemed impossible in the short time since he had ridden away from old Mason's shack with the five ten-dollar bills that he had come so far—far indeed from the lonely homestead in the river-breaks. He had fallen short of his goal: the coveted championship. But only temporarily. The National Association would award him the honour. Then his ambition would be realized.

A world champion! And over Harmon's protest. Damn Harmon! Still, Harmon had given him this —this glorious vista of mountain and plain spread out like a painting about him.

The trip from town the night before had been without incident. He and Barrington had ridden the ten miles together. Judy had come on with the rest by car.

The crowd had waited up for his arrival. There had been coffee and sandwiches in the great dining-room for the guests who straggled in all night. He had been the centre of attraction—a thing that embarrassed him. Apparently there was no help for it; if, indeed, he wanted to be spared the adulation of the crowd, which, for all his nervousness, he sometimes doubted.

He had tried to talk with Judy. But Alice, in a manner that struck him as selfish instead of a genuine desire to be with him, had monopolized his time until finally he had begged off and gone to bed. It even seemed as though she took a secret delight in his embarrassment as she led him about introducing him to her guests.

That was all past now. More than a thousand dollars was tucked away in the leather wallet in his pocket beneath his chaps—winnings from his first rodeo. And, in addition, the saddle he had ridden out from town was a silver-mounted affair. He chuckled at the thought of the envy it would have created among the boys who rode the round-ups back on the Cheyenne River. The spurs he now wore were inlaid with gold and silver. His boots were fancy-stitched. The buckle of the belt that circled his lean waist was gold. He would have his picture taken with the saddle immediately—to show old Mason and the cowboys up home.

He had passed the time on the ride out from town stroking the stamped leather of the new saddle lovingly, or riding sidewise that he might the better see the glorious rigging. A new Navajo blanket added to the luxuriousness of the outfit, and a silver-mounted bridle with a bit-chain that tinkled musically. It clinked a merry tune as he rode—a tune that fitted in with the happiness that welled up within him.

He walked away from the bunkhouse presently towards the barns: low, long, rambling structures that struck him in odd comparison to the lean-to, sod-roofed shack at old Mason's place. Many a rancher out in the sage-brush would have been delighted with a house half as good as those barns that sheltered Harmon's saddle-horses.

Now the infant sun was tipping the Casper mountains behind him: massive granite shafts rearing into the heavens, the dark of their cañons creeping away before the light of day. A plaintive whine came to his ears: the glad song of the pines stirring lazily far up in the gloomy reaches.

Everything was green up there—more shades of green than he had ever before realized existed—the dark sombre green of pine and spruce, the lighter green buckbrush, the vivid green of aspen. And over the cañons lay a soft haze growing bluer, thinner as sunlight routed the clinging shadows of dawn.

Out beyond, where the broad prairie floor ran to the rolling hills of the Laramie River, the country was buff as it was at home. And the sage was grey. That sage made him lonely. For what, he still did not know. But of a sudden he did know that he had loved the idle hours of staring out across the flats back on the Cheyenne River. He had loved that country—loved everything but the soul-freezing loneliness. Even here he was lonely —strangely lonely now.

At the barn he turned to look back. The Cross Anchor dude ranch spread out like a miniature city about him. A broad cottonwood-lined avenue between two rows of neat log cabins, each with a rough stone fire-place. From a few of the cabins rose spirals of smoke.

At the head of the gravelled street was the main ranch-house—a two-storey pile of logs that reminded him of pictures he had seen of lodges in big parks. On the second floor was a rough-hewn veranda on which opened countless dormers with French doors, each flashing blindingly as they caught up the reflection of the morning sun. On the porch beneath were rustic rockers and gay Indian blankets. It looked cool and inviting. Already a grey-haired woman was at her knitting while she rocked monotonously, pausing from time to time to look out across the prairies, vivid now in the young light. He recalled having met that woman the night before: a Mrs. Erick Van Ressalder, of New York, a dowager with a once-pretty face, a coiffure that belonged on a model in a beauty-shop window, and a tight-laced figure that reminded him of grain-sacks in the feed-barns back home.

From the great kitchen which he had glimpsed —tiled, nickel-plated, modern to the last detail—came the rattle of pots and pans, the whistling of a boy laying the tables with snow-white linen, gleaming glass and silverware. The aroma of coffee and bacon as they drifted out on the morning breeze set him to sniffing eagerly. From memory he caught a whiff of coffee on a round-up, seemed to hear cowboys grumbling as they rolled out of their tarp-beds in the dawn to tug on damp boots and drop cross-legged on the ground to growl over their food. But at this moment the life he once had known was far behind, a sort of hazy dream.

He swung open the barn door, entered. Nickering reached his ears—a pleasant sound. A nickering pony always struck a responsive chord within him. Horses were so like people—friendly if one let them be.

He went on inside, stopped for a moment to stroke the outstretched nose of the nearest animal, which nuzzled him impatiently for its oats.

He fell to talking to the brutes—as he would talk to men—joking with them, teasing them as he went from manger to manger, finally to pour the grain into their feed-boxes as they coaxed. A stifled laugh brought him about guiltily. At the far end of the runway stood Judy Barrington, rocking with suppressed laughter. Grey flushed.

"Good morning," he managed to gulp out.

"Good morning." She came forward quickly to lay a hand on his arm at the hurt expression in his eyes. "Forgive me, I just couldn't help it. I wasn't laughing at you, honestly—just at the way you were talking to these horses, as though they were babies. Imagine Grey Sage, crack bronc-rider, talking baby talk to a barn full of half-ton horses!" She went off again in a gale of laughter —tinkling, musical laughter. But he did not join in it. He was too conscious of her hand on his arm. The strange emotions of the night before were engulfing him, for which he was sorry. His own thoughts were erecting a barrier between them—a barrier he seemed utterly incapable of surmounting.

"Horses are just like folks to me," he found himself explaining sheepishly. "I've been raised with them, as other men are raised with boys or girls."

She glanced at him—a strange look, as though she were undecided whether his innocence was a pose or natural. For an instant their gazes locked. Hers was the first to fall. But not before he had seen her in a new and searching way. Those lustrous brown eyes, in their frankness, their utter honesty, were, he was positive, incapable of falsehood. The sun streaming through the barn windows was stringing gold through her hair. It had a reddish tinge. Still not red—that was for her cheeks, in which healthy colour played. And, he noticed, she was still without make-up of any sort. The redness of her full, arched lips was natural. He thrilled to her, a woman who could look like this so early in the morning. The women he had seen around the ranches had always appeared so unkempt, so untidy—almost slovenly.

For all he could do, his eyes roved boldly along her. She was garbed in a brown silk shirt that clung caressingly to her full-breasted figure. Small she was—tiny was the word that flashed into his mind. She stood now at full height, yet only reached his shoulders. He was looking down on her. His eyes rested for a moment on the open V at her throat. The startling whiteness of that throat made him conscious that he was staring. His eyes flashed down to her beautifully moulded hips in snug-fitting jodhpurs, dainty little booted feet. Her garb was elegant in a quiet way—rich, worn with distinction.

For all the time it seemed he had consumed in devouring her with hungry eyes, it was but a flashing glance, his mind racing far faster than his gaze. She took a step nearer, was looking up at him.

"Let's just be friends," she said, an oddly husky note in her voice.

"Why . . . yes . . ." he stammered. "That is . . . I hope . . ."

She skipped over to the oat-bin, filled a measure, came dancing back to pour it into the box of a softly wickering pony. "Friends . . . the greatest thing in the world, cowboy. Get to work. What are you standing there for? You've got a whole flock of doting mammas to take out for a canter this morning. It's a canter now. No more loping or busting the breeze for you."

Her rare good humour swept away his embarrassment. Still he was vaguely aware that under the code he had known there was something wrong in her being out here working with him at feeding the horses before the others were about. He hated to mention it. With the quick intuition of a woman, she read it in his eyes.

"It's all right," she said, going back to the oat-bin, bending over until one shapely leg was sticking high in the air. "That's why I asked that we be friends, so we really could enjoy each other's company." His silence brought her up quickly, her ringlets tossed in wild disarray. "We can be . . . can't we?"

Again their eyes met. Something passed between them—some strange, unexplainable thing that frightened him.

"Yes." But he knew he lied. He never could be merely friends with Judy Barrington. There was something about her—perhaps it was because he had been denied the companionship of women so long. At least, he tried thus to reason with himself as they stood looking at one another. Perhaps . . .

Old Mason's warning sounded in his ears.

"Never steal another man's critters . . . or his wife."

Steal this pretty woman! The thought was so ridiculous that a smile pulled his lips from their grim set. But it vanished instantly. There was no smile in the eyes of the girl that met his so frankly.

She was coming forward slowly, the tilted measure of oats leaving a trail behind. A mist of tears sprang into her eyes. He blinked in amazement. She was crying. For what? Had he said or done something? He didn't understand her, neither her words nor her emotions.

"Why can't we be just friends?" He blurted out the thing in his mind. His voice was hoarse with a sudden dryness—a feverish dryness that seemed to extend to every part of him, burning him, leaving him a little dizzy, reckless. Never before had he been so close to a woman who seemed to fire his blood at a glance. True, he had seen other women: thousands of them in the last few days—women who had deliberately tried to stop him, enter into a conversation; girls who had pulled their cars over to the curb, invited him to ride. But none of them had been a woman such as this—a woman who, without speaking, was filling him with an emotion so powerful it all but robbed him of the power of speech, certainly the ability to think coherently.

"We can . . . can't . . ." Her eyes fell. The oat-measure dropped from her fingers to scatter grain. The unfed horses stared, nickered accusing protest. He stifled an insane desire to gather her in his arms—lay a hand on her shoulder that suddenly had sagged dejectedly. "We can if we—"

She was swaying. Impelled by some motive that frightened him, he started to reach for her. Somehow he knew that she would be in his arms, that he loved her, had loved her from the moment he had seen her at the chute from the careening back of Widow-Maker, that here was the ideal he had built up in his fancy.

For all he could do, his arm went round her shoulder. An electric thrill raced through him. He knew that she felt it too, for she was coming closer. He blinked to shut out the alluring vision, cursed himself for his mad folly. Yet he was helpless in the power of this gripping sensation. His other hand went round her waist. Her eyes lifted. There was a stifled sob on her lips. Her quivering body was against him. Her own arms started up.

"I beg your pardon," came from the doorway. "I didn't know . . . Perhaps I am intruding."

They tore apart, whirled guiltily. Regarding them with accusing eyes was Alice Harmon.

Chapter IX

The three stood in embarrassed silence. Judy Barrington's face was flaming. Grey Sage flushed darkly. Alice alone retained her composure. She smiled in a friendly way—a thing for which Grey's heart went out to her.

"A horse, a horse! My kingdom for a horse," she quoted blithely, coming on into the barn. "How are you, dear?" She placed an arm about Judy, who was still speechless, although her poise had returned. "You look sweet enough to kiss this morning. Doesn't she, Grey?" There was banter, a challenge in her eyes. He was positive she was laughing at him. At the moment he hated her. But he had no one to blame but himself. It was his fault Judy had been implicated. Yet what had she been doing in the barn? Was he responsible that she set his blood to pounding?

"You want a horse, Miss Harmon?" he asked, starting away.

"I want *my* horse, Mr. Sage," she corrected, skipping alongside of him. "Jumbo there . . . that sorrel. I always take a ride before breakfast. Judy and I. She seems to have beaten me out here this morning."

Grey dared a glance at Judy, who had not

moved. There was that in her gaze he could not fathom; she was trying to tell him something with her eyes.

Alice pointed out the sorrel, Jumbo, showed him her outfit, stood by while he tossed on and cinched the saddle. Replacing the halter with a bridle, he led the horse from the stall.

"I guess Judy isn't going this morning," Alice said as the girl turned and left the barn without a word. "I hate to ride alone. Won't you come with me?"

"I'd like to," Grey said, at a loss for anything else to say. "But a common wrangler doesn't ride with the boss's niece! Besides, I've got work to do."

"Dude ranches are about the only place on earth where everyone is on an equal footing." She laughed happily. "Wrangler or magnate, it's all the same. And on the Cross Anchor the top wrangler takes orders from no one but the boss's niece." The tone of the last was a little too patronizing, he thought. "I'll have the other boys do the feeding."

"But I want to," he put in. "I've always been around horses. They're friends to me."

"Saddle up. We're going for a ride." Her words smacked strongly of a command.

For a moment it occurred to him to tell her to go to the devil. Her tone, which seemed to admit of no refusal, angered him. He stood staring after her as she led her horse towards the door. There she paused to look back. "Come on," she said coaxingly. "It's too fine to miss a ride before breakfast. They'll be shouting for us if we don't get started quickly. Jerry!" she hailed another cowboy crossing the yard. "You feed the horses mornings from now on."

Hating himself for his easy acquiescence, yet unable to see how the thing was to be avoided, Grey tossed his new silver-mounted saddle on his own pony and led it forth. With the inherent courtesy of the cowboy—who, while he may lack polish, still possesses a rare chivalry—he helped Alice into her saddle, swung up himself. He set spurs to his horse, whirled about. He caught sight of Judy walking back towards her cabin slowly, head down.

At the home pasture he dismounted, dropped the gate. Alice turned towards the prairie into the face of the rising sun. He swung up, rowelled alongside of her. They rode in silence, each busy with their own thoughts. His thoughts were of Judy. He berated himself for his actions, half fearful that because of a momentary emotion he had lost her friendship almost as it was born.

"You're in love with Judy Barrington, aren't you?" Alice asked with a suddenness that startled him.

"No," he denied. "I never laid eyes on her until yesterday."

"You're a mighty fast worker. If I hadn't come into the barn just when I did you'd have kissed Judy. You're lucky it was me instead of Hugh."

"I'm not that kind of a fellow." The eyes he turned upon her were deeply troubled. "You believe me, don't you?"

She looked at him puzzled—an inscrutable, soul- searching gaze. It had been a look such as this that had thrown him into a panic at the banquet.

She reached out, laid a hand over his on the saddle-horn.

"Too much, I guess. But—I was thinking of you. You don't want to get mixed up with . . ." She flushed.

"Well." He tried to keep the coldness out of his voice, at the same time thrilling to the contact of her hand on his as the horses jogged along side by side. He made no attempt to understand himself. Here, in the space of a few hours, he had met two women who stood out above all the rest—two women who appeared even lovelier than the dream-creatures he had pictured in his fancy. It was Judy who had slipped into his mind to replace the woman of his dreams. But Alice, too, set his blood and nerves hammering. She was prettier than Judy, in a cold, frozen way. And he made no attempt to deny the thrill her nearness gave him.

He looked at her frankly in the morning light.

She was as well groomed as she had been the night before—a picture torn from a magazine, in black jodhpurs, a bright red silk shirt, her black hair gleaming, unruffled by the breeze. She sat her saddle like a veteran, a slim girl who would arrest the attention of any man. Still, she was almost too well garbed. Too much attention had been paid to her toilet. The fragrance of her reminded him of a hot-house—a closed room stacked with flowers all blending their odours until it had become stifling, sickeningly sweet. Beneath her eyes he noticed darkened rings with delicate blue veins that gave them an unnatural bigness and depth. Beautiful, that face. But, he was afraid of her: afraid of her beauty, her coldness, her aloofness. He wondered if it was not because he had never before known a woman of her type—a woman of wealth whose command could send vassals running.

Patrician . . . somewhere he had heard the word. It brought to his mind visions of bejewelled women of ancient times. After all, what difference did it make? Women had been the same since the dawn of history—beguiling, scheming, ruthless. Why should man fear them? He had| no fear of the pounding hoofs of a half-ton outlaw. Yet this woman?

"Judy isn't happy with Barrington," Alice was saying in a low, husky voice that he could scarcely catch. She pulled her hand away, fell to brushing the broadcloth jodhpur where it lay caressingly against a rounded thigh.

"I didn't know," he mumbled. "I don't even know what happened there at the barn . . . what I was thinking."

"I do," she said pointedly—too pointedly. "Judy Barrington is a very charming woman, a woman few men can overlook. And she is a great rider."

"She is?"

"One of the finest in the country. If Hugh would let her, she would be woman bronc-riding champion of the world. She was born and raised on a ranch here in Wyoming."

"She's not like the run of ranch-girls. She's educated."

"Judy and I went to school together in the East. We've been pals for years. Dad owned this ranch. Judy's father was his foreman. They both died. Uncle John sold out and came to run this place for me. Shortening of range, the depression, which knocked the bottom out of the cattle market, left us on a limb. Uncle John turned the Cross Anchor into a dude ranch. I just came back this summer. And"—she gave him another of those bewildering glances that left him more and more puzzled—"I know I'm going to like it here now."

"Why?" he blurted out before he thought.

"You'd be surprised." Her tone was bantering.

He did not press her. He wanted to hear more

of Judy, even though he felt like a cad prying into her affairs. But if she was unhappy with Barrington—and apparently Alice intended to tell him, for she was chattering on familiarly, as though they had been friends for years.

"Judy and I came back from the East together. She had decided to remain there and accept a position as a confidential secretary to a million-aire—a wonderful opportunity. Her father left her just enough to complete her schooling. But she's like you—she couldn't stay away from the West. She loves horses, wants to be with them every minute. You're liable to find her down at the barn even at night. But"—she looked at him with an amazing frankness—"I'd be careful if I were you. Hugh Barrington is jealous."

He flushed in spite of himself.

"Guess he needn't watch me." At the moment he meant it. Yet the remark struck him as puerile, a defence offered for nothing but his own conscience.

"Don't be too sure." Alice made no attempt to disguise the warning in her voice. "Judy is a mighty attractive girl. She's just a bride. Hugh, many times a champion bronc-rider, has been uncle's foreman for a long time. Top hands on dude ranches, you know, can just about take their pick of the girls who come out. There seems to be something about them women can't resist. We'd only been back a short time when Judy married Hugh. I knew she didn't love him. She was struck with the glamour of him, of any champion cowboy, of being back in this big country she loves. He swept her off her feet."

"Too bad," he muttered inanely.

"For Judy, yes . . . perhaps for you."

"I wish you wouldn't keep including me. After all, I haven't done anything. I didn't marry her. If she's unhappy, I'm sorry. Still, I don't reckon it is any of my affair."

Again Alice leaned over in her saddle, placed her hand on his—an unconsciously intimate gesture that completely destroyed his calm.

"It's always a man's affair when a woman as pretty as Judy is unhappy with her husband," she said in a low voice, "because it is inevitable that some day they will part. They can't go on with the thing for ever. Hugh idolizes her, but he's insanely jealous. And from what I saw in the barn this morning, he has a right to be."

"Please." Again she had him pleading.

"Forgive me, I didn't mean to be catty. But I . . . I owe you considerable. You saved my life yesterday. I shan't forget it."

They jogged along in silence, the only sound that of the prairie life stirring to wakefulness in the warming flood of morning sunlight.

But now they had topped a great table-land. He drew rein to survey the vista spread out before them.

Endless acres of grey sage and greasewood, tangled, chaotic bad-lands that melted away into the haze of a far horizon. Here and there on the vast expanse rose up box-topped buttes, sinister-looking, weirdly-shaped. Unconsciously he threw back his shoulders, breathed deeply of the sage-tanged air. That breath soothed the heavy feeling that lay upon him, a constantly recurring feeling that he never seemed able to understand.

Judy! The name persisted in stealing into his mind, her image kept flashing before his eyes—an alluring picture that left within him a glad feeling even when his thoughts were of other things. So she was unhappy? Yet there was nothing he could do about it. After that morning his presence on the ranch would not help. He had money. He could go back to the Cheyenne River, or go on following the rodeos. There was Calgary yet, and Salinas. He'd always wanted to go to Calgary—wanted to take a try at the big stampede and the North American bucking championship up there. Why remain here longer?

"Reckon I'll see your uncle, and just be moving along," he said.

"Moving along? You don't mean leave the Cross Anchor?"

"Yes."

"Are you going to let a woman run you away from the first big thing you ever did in your life?" There was unmistakable scorn in her voice.

"No woman is running me away," he defended lamely. "I want to take a shot at Calgary or Salinas."

She rode close now—too close for his peace of mind.

"Don't be a quitter right from the start," she said earnestly. "Women aren't worth it. This position you have with us will mean your fortune —an independent living for the rest of your life. As quickly as I can, I'm going to give you Hugh Barrington's place as foreman. Eventually Uncle John will want to retire and turn over the active management of the ranch."

"Then what?" he demanded savagely.

"The firm of Sage and Harmon would sound well as owners of the Cross Anchor, wouldn't it?"

"Meaning?"

"Grey Sage and Alice Harmon," boldly.

He didn't exactly get her drift. Yet, for all the things that rushed into his mind, he managed to hold his tongue.

"It's the foot-itch, I reckon." He was hedging. He knew it. But he couldn't check himself. "Now that I've made the break from the range, I can't seem to settle down. When I get a smell of sage like this"—he swept the prairie with an outstretched arm, a gesture that set his horse to shying—"I just can't stay put. It seems like I've got to keep going."

"Running away from yourself," she said in a cold tone that both startled and nettled him.

"Running away from myself?"

"Yes . . . from your own fear . . . from Judy . . . from people . . . and from me."

"From you?"

"Yes."

"Why . . . you?"

"Because you are afraid of me. Aren't you?"

"Yes."

"Why should you be?"

"We aren't of the same folks." He stared out across the flats dreamily. "You've got education. I've had almost no schooling. You've got polish. Me . . . I'm just a cowboy. But why should we go into those things?"

"Because I want you to. I love a champion. A champion has something the other fellow lacks. Men look alike and act alike. There's something different underneath. Otherwise they'd all be champions."

"But I'm not a champion," he blurted out bitterly. "I tried—I've always wanted it, always dreamed of it. I couldn't grade up. There was something lacking."

"Your failure was due to Uncle John's protest, simply because he is a poor loser. But don't worry. The world is full of poor losers like him.

And the world is short on champions like you. You'll come into your own. It's born into you. You'll be champion bronc-rider yet."

"I reckon it will be breakfast time, won't it?" He changed the subject abruptly.

"I reckon it will, cowboy," she smiled. "And I'm just plenty hungry. How about you?"

"So hungry I could eat a skunk, if it was skinned and dressed out right."

They reined about, galloped back to the ranch in silence.

Chapter X

The days following were an amazing whirl for Grey Sage. Everything was strange—the carefully groomed guests, their talk, their mannerisms —until he was a little bewildered. And then there was Judy. Although since their meeting in the barn she had obviously avoided him, never did he succeed in driving her from his mind. Occasion-ally he got a glimpse of her on the veranda or at the table, glanced up to surprise her eyes on him. The thing he saw in her eyes puzzled him the more.

Alice was with him at every opportunity. Had she been less companionable, he would have dodged her. Instead he found himself looking forward to their rides together, found more pleasure in her company than he cared to admit to himself. Still, there was always that coldness about her he feared. Rarely he managed to chip beneath the frigid exterior and see the real girl, buoyant, vivacious. Save for those glimpses, he could not break down her reserve, neither could he overcome his tormenting fear of her.

He often wondered what she had meant that day of their first ride by saying that he was running away from himself. He strove diligently to discover what she saw that he could not. He was no different from any one else. He wasn't running away from anything. Yet, he had been driven from the homestead on the river—the thing he had always wanted—by haunting loneliness. And now he was planning to leave the Cross Anchor because of . . . Judy or Alice? He didn't know which.

He made no attempt to delude himself with a belief that he did not care for Judy. He did, with a depth that was making him morose, melancholic with thought of her. The emotion was becoming so strong he scarcely dared look at her, for fear someone would detect it in his glance.

He had written to old Mason, had repaid his friend's loan with interest, told him of his job, of his victory at the Arapahoe Stampede— uncertain though it was—had mentioned both Judy and Alice. An answer, scrawled in pencil, had come back promptly. Homely philosophy filled the pages. One part etched itself into Grey's mind. Old Mason, too, had written concerning Judy, casually.

"Remember what I told you about stealing . . . I know what you are up against . . . I can read it in the things you didn't write. Be honourable, kid. Don't steal a man's wife, any more than you would his critters. By stealing his wife I don't mean loping up, throwing her on a horse and riding away with her. There are other ways. To steal a woman's love away from her husband is just as bad as though you ran off with her."

That part of the letter had worried Grey.

Hugh Barrington he had found to be an excellent companion, although at times the loud-voiced cowboy jarred on his nerves. Barrington, a natural foreman for a dude ranch, was always shouting and wise-cracking with the men, patting the dowagers on the shoulders and chucking the pretty girls under the chin.

"If I were that pretty little Mrs. Barrington," Grey overheard two women remarking one morning as they rocked on the veranda, "I'd be jealous of the way her husband treats these other girls. His actions are positively scandalous. He's always going on with some of them."

"Mrs. Barrington doesn't care, if you ask me," came the reply that seemed to freeze Grey. "It only takes half an eye to see she is head over heels in love with that rider, Grey Sage."

Grey had cleared his throat to make known his presence, passed on, head in the air. But he felt the eyes of the women boring into his back. He squared his shoulders in an all-too-obvious attempt to appear unperturbed.

He cursed the scandalous tongues that wagged about the ranch, especially those of the old women who seemed to spend their time whispering innuendos. He wondered what they came to a dude ranch for anyway? They did nothing but sit and knit and gossip about the younger people. But if it was common gossip that Judy had so much as looked at him, the least he could do would be to leave.

His periodic decisions to ride away were counterbalanced by thought of leaving Judy . . . and Alice. Other girls there were on the ranch— no less than a dozen—pretty, polished daughters of the East who followed him wherever he went with admiring glances and who made no effort to conceal their fascination. Yet among all of them Judy was the one unapproachable, the one untouchable. He sometimes wondered if that were not the reason he wanted her so badly, with the natural desire of humans for something unattainable.

The work Grey found almost too simple to be called work. Had he been able to do it alone, it would have been a constant round of pleasantry. But, as it was, he always had half a dozen girls and men on whom he was forced to dance attendance. He led them on rides across the prairies or back into the mountains, guided them, explained everything from horses to cougars, helped them with their saddles and their mounts. The men needed little such attention. But the girls seemed continually to require his help with a cinch or a stirrup-guard. He waited upon them patiently, although many times after examining a strap that was causing trouble he found nothing wrong, and looked up inquiringly into dancing eyes that as much as told him the whole affair had been a ruse.

Few of the older women rode the bridle-paths, for which he was thankful. He did not like them. He had met them and dodged away from any conversation with them as quickly as he had been able. Particularly Mrs. Van Ressalder, who epitomized everything that was catty to Grey. She, of all the rest, always found time to be on the look-out for something she could turn into scandal, as she rocked monotonously on the veranda and stared rudely at every one who passed. She had a ready counterpart in Mrs. Worthington Truebolt, of Philadelphia. Once they had started their morsels of scandal travelling, they seemed to be on hand to catch any other choice tidbits they could warp into malicious gossip.

Apart from these two, Grey found most of the crowd congenial, although they were clannish— a thing that many times embarrassed him. However, he had to do with only those who spent their time riding, so it worried him little.

The thing that was to bring an unexpected end to this fool's paradise of his—which he was never quite able to understand—came about in the corral one evening. Barrington and he had been riding for horses. They had driven in a large bunch, thrown them into the round corrals. In the snorting, kicking herd was Widow-Maker.

"Getting ready for the show," Hugh said. "Here's where you earn your pay, cowboy."

Grey only glanced at him.

"Once a month we put on a rodeo for the guests. Greaser ropes some calves. Jerry and the other boys wrestle some steers. The top wrangler busts a bronc. Makes a hit with the old ladies, who demand more excitement than the girls. The men bust their galluses to shake hands with you after you climb down."

"At least it will break the monotony," Grey said.

"You feel that way, too?" Barrington regarded him quizzically. "Never thought the way you've been rushing Alice you were the kind who had the foot-itch."

"The whole damned layout gives me a pain in the neck, if you ask me," Grey exploded. "Getting out in the morning, showing a flock of dizzy dames how to sit up straight in a saddle, riding along a trail you've followed every hour for days, helping women up, helping women down. I'm fed up with women. I'd like a few more cows and horses and a little more sage-brush, instead of so damned much skirt and silk stocking."

"You and me both, cowboy," Barrington laughed. "Thought I'd go nuts the first year I was with this dude spread. And I'm not stuck on it yet. Got an idea working in the back of my head. Going to do some riding at the rodeos myself this fall. Then a wild horse string of my own. I'm dickering for a string that isn't to be sneezed at. A has-been champ like me and a coming champ like you could go places together with a wild bunch."

"Sounds good to me," Grey said. "But you're set here."

"Like hell I am! A bronc-rider isn't set anywhere. Think it over, cowboy."

They had gone on to complete their chores, then to the bunkhouse to the showers and to garb themselves in flashy chaps and shirts. For they never wore the same clothes around the house they wore near the barns. The odour of the barnyard offended the dowagers. Every one dressed for dinner. The Cross Anchor cowboys appeared in flaming range regalia.

That evening the guests assembled in the great living-room. A pitch-knot fire crackled in the fire-place; even though it was summer a chill crept down from the mountains with twilight.

Harmon himself was mingling with the crowd that night—an unusual thing, for he seldom came forth in the evening. Presently he shouted for attention.

"I have a treat for you, folks," he boomed in his deep voice. "To-morrow, you know, we stage our monthly rodeo. This time you're going to see our crack bronc-rider, Grey Sage, top off a horse. And that horse . . ." he looked round until he captured Grey's curious gaze, ". . . is to be Widow-Maker, the animal he attempted to ride at Arapahoe for the world championship."

Grey jerked with violently straining muscles. But he said nothing. Alice—his constant companion it seemed—leaned over, took him by the arm.

"Uncle John will never be satisfied that you made a qualified ride in the finals at Arapahoe," she whispered in a voice that angered him unreasonably. "That's why he picked Widow-Maker—that and the thousand-dollar bet."

"He kept me from a world championship by his belly-aching. But what thousand-dollar bet?"

"Have you forgotten?"

For the moment he had. Now he remembered. He had bet Harmon a thousand dollars at Arapahoe he could ride any horse he had any time or any place.

"You never want to forget anything with Uncle John," Alice was saying. "He never does. He's never forgiven you for making that ride. It spoils the perfect record of his prize-bucking horse."

"Nice fellow," Grey snorted contemptuously. "Never did like him, and never will."

"It's mutual," she assured him in a tone that stung.

"But a man doesn't have to stay around!" he flung at her, wondering why he should vent his anger upon her in such a childish manner.

"Not if he is the kind who runs away from himself . . . who is afraid of . . . well, just being afraid."

He slammed up from his seat. In a dozen strides he had crossed the room to halt beside Harmon. The rancher turned.

"Howdy, Sage. Suppose you heard my announcement. You recall our bet?" He raised his voice. "Another little surprise, folks. Back at Arapahoe, Sage bet a thousand dollars he could ride any horse I had. He's riding Widow-Maker to-morrow for that thousand dollars. I suppose you have your money ready?"

Grey squared off to stand spread-legged for a moment, prey to a consuming anger. Flame flecked his eyes. His fists balled. A moment of breathless silence settled down, a moment pregnant with possibility of trouble. The buzz of conversation ceased. The pitch knots blazing in the fire-place crackled loudly in the sudden still-ness. Once Grey's fist started up. Never before had he been so furiously mad, not only at Harmon, but also at the suave, cool-voiced Alice. It was she, not Harmon, who had goaded him to this unreasonable fury. They were attempting to hold him up to ridicule, were deliberately forcing his hand before all these guests. Hot words flew to his lips. They were never uttered. A cool little hand had come to rest on his fist.

"Steady, cowboy," came a whispered voice—a voice that carried far more than a pleading tone. "He's trying to make you mad. Take it on the chin and grin. Let it work out itself."

No need to ask to whom that voice belonged. It thrilled him now as it had thrilled him when first he had heard it. Of late the torment had been because he did not hear enough of it. His balled fists opened. His hand closed about tiny fingers. A quick pressure was his reward. Then Judy Barrington moved up beside him.

The girl's nearness assuaged his anger. After all, she was the only one he cared about. But Barrington . . . he felt guilty. Hugh was directly opposite in the crowd, lifting a cocktail to his lips. If he had heard he gave no sign.

When Grey spoke it was with a thin smile. And a new light had replaced the anger in his eyes. He found his wallet, handed his carefully guarded bank-roll over to Judy.

"Mrs. Barrington will make a good stake-holder," he said, with an evenness that amazed him. "My thousand is posted . . . that I can ride Widow-Maker or any other horse in your string. Let's see your money, Harmon."

The ready acquiescence of the cowboy plainly nonplussed Harmon.

"I'll write a cheque," he said sourly.

Came to Grey's lips to refuse. A look from Judy silenced his protest.

"The rules?" he found himself asking. "I presume they will be the same as at the regular rodeos?"

"At our rodeos, which are merely for the entertainment of our guests, we haven't any rules." Harmon's voice carried a peculiarly gloating note. "Our riders come out of the corrals and ride their mounts down."

"But I won't . . ." Grey started.

"Yes, you will." It was Alice who spoke from his shoulder. "You'll ride Widow-Maker and make Uncle John like it." For all the finality of her tone there was also encouragement that for the moment made him love her. She slipped her arm through his. Judy was no longer beside him. She had moved away as Alice came up.

"Ride Widow-Maker down!" It would be the ride of his life. And he had his doubts. He was afraid of Widow-Maker—for the first time in his life afraid of a horse. Came to him the advice of old Mason.

"When you get afraid of a horse, quit . . . that's when a cowboy gets hurt."

But now there was no alternative. Harmon, for revenge, was deliberately trying to hold him up to ridicule. Why? It was Alice who supplied the reason.

"Uncle John is angry because I . . . I like you," she whispered.

"It isn't any crime to like a person, is it?" he demanded.

Before she replied she pulled him gently away into the crowd which, the moment of tenseness past, had resumed its interrupted conversation.

"No, but Uncle John thinks I . . . love you," she said softly.

Unconsciously impelled by the girl's guiding hand on his arm, he had moved outside on the veranda. They walked over to the railing to stand looking out into the night.

A full moon, like a great lantern, hung on the skyline. Moons such as this always increased his loneliness. He never knew why. As a youngster he had lain on his back out on the prairies and watched such moons. They set him to dreaming of far places, seemed to touch a chord within him that made him want either to cry or sing.

Now the moon was throwing a silver sheen over the flats, bringing up the brush like eerie figures of a nightmare—great sinister phantoms in the effulgent glow. Somewhere far across the arid reaches a cow was bawling. From the shadowed foothills came an answering bawl, drifting end-lessly, like his present thoughts, across the chasm of the night.

Then again he was aware that the girl was close beside him. He glanced at her. Her face was upturned. That face was like a painting he had seen . . . a beautiful creature . . . a madonna . . . almost too perfect. He could feel the fingers, that still clutched his arm, trembling.

When he spoke it was with a husky, uncertain note. Never had his voice failed him this way before. Only once, at the stampede banquet at Arapahoe. Then his knees had been shaking. Now he never felt stronger, although his voice persisted in breaking.

"But you aren't in love with me," he got out. "Are you?" Why he turned the assertion into a question he did not know.

The answer that came back left him breathless.

"Yes, I am." The girl's eyes fell. She turned away to stare off across the moonlit prairies. But her body did not move.

Her confession—her very tone was a confession —confused him. He said nothing, for the simple reason he did not know what to say. But her words momentarily made him forget his fear of her, his fear of her coldness. He took courage. He could scarcely realize he was the same Grey Sage—Grey Sage of the little homestead far up in the lonely sweeps of Wyoming. Here beside him was a lovely woman. She was clinging to his arm. And—he caught his breath sharply— tears were glistening in her eyes gazing out over the flats. Real tears, he knew. He melted under them.

Impelled by a wild impulse, he drew his arm from her hand, laid it across her shoulder.

"You . . . love . . . me?" he whispered hoarsely.

"I loved you from the moment I was in your

arms after you'd saved me from that bull." Her voice was broken, uncertain. It was evident that she was ashamed of her show of emotion. "Can't you understand?" She whirled suddenly. Her arms went round his neck. "Kiss me, Grey!"

Once before Grey Sage had experienced a similar sensation: the day he had ridden Widow-Maker at Arapahoe, after his leg had crashed against the gatepost coming out of the chute. The pain had set him to shaking his head to clear the cobwebs from his brain. His brain was whirling now. Not from pain, but with the same bewildering sensation that left him incapable of coherent thought. Alice Harmon was asking him, Grey Sage—a cowboy from a Wyoming homestead—to kiss her!

Before he could think clearly, the girl was in his arms. He was crushing her to him, raining kisses down upon her mouth. She was clinging to him, her soft, pliant body melting against him.

"Alice . . . Alice . . ." he was murmuring brokenly. "I didn't . . . know . . . I . . ."

"Grey"—her voice, languidly delicious, seemed to be coming to him from far, far away—"if you'll ride that horse to-morrow, I'll marry you in spite of uncle."

"Marry me?" It took a moment for him to understand. But he couldn't think. Why try? She was in his arms, close against him. He never wanted to break the contact. "Marry me?"

A stifled sob broke the spell, brought them about. Judy arose from a chair on the veranda. They were directly in her line of vision. With a little cry, Alice fled. Grey stood alone. Judy came over to him. She gazed up into his eyes, which still did not seem to see alright.

"She'll marry you if you make that ride, Grey Sage," Judy was saying fiercely. "Alice Harmon, the heiress, will marry you. You're made. Do you realize? You're made . . . I . . ." She wilted, shoulders sagging. He reached for her, his mind still in a whirl. But she pulled away.

"No," she snapped. "I made a fool of myself once. But not again. She'll marry you. . . ." Her voice broke. ". . . She loves you . . . I . . . Don't stand there staring like a sap."

He jerked violently.

"But, Judy," he gulped, "I don't want—"

"What do you want?" she demanded. "All the women in the world? Alice Harmon said she would marry you if you made that ride. As for me . . . if you don't, I'll . . . I'll . . . slap your face." She whirled and was gone, leaving him staring after her.

Chapter XI

A scowling, worried Grey Sage pulled on his chaps at daybreak the following morning. He strapped spurs on booted heels, made his way out into the dawn, tormented with recollection of the happenings of the night before. His thousand dollars—the money he had earned, the most money he had ever had at one time—was staked on his ability to re-ride the brute on which he knew, through a lucky break, he had qualified in the Arapahoe finals. If only the Association had ruled favourably upon that championship ride before he attempted this one. At least there would be the satisfaction of knowing he had attained the coveted goal. If Widow-Maker threw him now, Harmon would publicize the fact to further his protest against the Arapahoe ride.

His nerves were jumpy. The events of the preceding evening had driven away sleep. He had rolled and tossed throughout the night. First it was Alice, her arms clinging about his neck, that had tormented his dreams. Then it was Judy. One stunning conclusion had come of the whole affair. He loved Judy Barrington. Alice? She swept him off his feet when he was near her. Still, he couldn't say that he didn't love her. He was fearful of her—fearful of her coldness, her money, her position in this world of wealth of which he knew nothing.

Within him persisted a warning that, no matter what his heart might dictate, Alice was not for him. With that warning recurred the words of old Mason—"Marry a girl of the West, your mother was of the East . . . this country is hell on women and broncs."

He smiled in spite of himself at the thought of Alice on his homestead as his wife. The smile faded quickly. There was only one who fitted that picture—little Judy. But Judy was married—unhappily, Alice had told him.

Alice . . . Judy. He tried to drive their images from his mind. One he loved, the other he feared. Yet, Alice's soft arms had been about his neck, her face upturned to his in the moonlight. Her whispered plea sounded again and again in his ears. "Kiss me, Grey . . . ride that horse and I'll marry you." Small wonder that his head was in a whirl, that he scarcely heard Barrington as he strode towards the barn.

The big foreman fell in alongside, hooked an arm through his—a friendly gesture. But, then, everything was friendly about Hugh.

"Coast, cowboy," the foreman was cautioning. "You're not riding for a championship now. You're riding to please a bunch of dudes who don't know whether you're doing a good job or a bad one. You aren't tied down by rules. Sink those spurs in from the first jump and go to town. That's the way I'd do it."

"But not the way I would." Grey whirled, immediately regretted his words at the look that crossed Barrington's face. "Forgive me. I didn't mean it that way. But I'm going to ride Widow-Maker straight up."

"Don't be a damned sap," Hugh exploded.

Grey started. Sap! That was the word Judy had used. "Don't stand there staring like a sap." He seemed again to hear her talking on the veranda the night before. Judy . . . Hugh Barrington's wife.

"What have you got to gain?" Hugh was saying. "A thousand bucks. Alice is worth a good many times that amount."

"What's that to you?" Grey demanded belligerently.

"Not a thing, cowboy." Barrington grinned. "But I'm not blind. Alice is crazy about you. This deal is the Old Man's. He's still sore at you for tromping Widow-Maker at Arapahoe—and for killing his prize bull. He'll never get over it. That's why he called this play . . . to show you up. But, my God, Judy and I don't mean to have you shown up by the vindictive old devil. Nor Alice doesn't either. She tried to get me to fix the horse, feed it poisoned grain—anything so you would win."

"I will win." A cold, brooding determination had come to Grey. Win he would, even if it cost him his life. He would show Harmon. He would buck down Widow-Maker, prove his ride at the stampede, his claim to the championship.

Strangely it wasn't of Alice he was thinking. It was of Judy. Again he seemed to hear her talking on the veranda. "Ride him or I'll slap your face!" He wondered what Barrington would say if he knew. He took secret delight in the knowledge that Barrington did not know. Yet, big Hugh had never hurt him.

"I won't coast," he said. "I'll give that damned snake-eye everything I've got. I'll kick him down."

"You will when you talk like that," Barrington said.

Grey Sage ignored the breakfast call. He wished he was on a round-up. Instead of those gongs he would hear a cook bellowing: "Come and get it, or I'll throw it out!" He never wanted to hear any more gongs; he'd had all the dude ranches he ever wanted to see, riding for the entertainment of a bunch of fatheads that didn't know a bad horse from one that could canter. Canter! He snorted disgustedly, cursed and fumed as he paced the yard waiting for the time when he could climb aboard Widow-Maker. Damn Harmon's soul! Once off the bronc, he'd make him eat everything he'd ever said. So

Harmon was opposed to his marriage with Alice? He'd show him about her, too!

An infinity of restless prowling. A crowd was collecting at the corrals. Dowagers in rustling silks, some with lorgnettes. How he hated those damned things! They always reminded him of a one-eyed man trying to cover up the imitation that didn't match the other pupil. The men, garbed in neatly pressed riding-breeches and black coats, made Grey think of pictures he had seen of hunters who followed the hounds. To hell with them too!—Even the big black cigars they rolled lovingly with their tongues annoyed him.

He reached for the makings in his shirt pocket, tapped tobacco into a paper, twisted a cigarette. He lighted it, flicked the match at the feet of one of the women staring at him with unconcealed admiration. She drew away. Grey smiled.

Then Barrington was calling for him. They had Widow-Maker eared down, blinded and saddled in the corral. Grey jerked his spur-straps a notch tighter, hoisted his chaps with his wrists. He strode out before them. Damn them all. They were there to gloat over him. But . . . there was Alice. The coldness in her eyes had vanished. There was something almost pathetic about her. And over there was Judy. She had a handkerchief to her mouth, as he had first seen her. No need for her to worry. He would ride Widow-Maker.

He crawled into the corral, was beside the bronc

that stood trembling, front legs spraddled, bowed belly almost touching the ground.

"Remember what I said, cowboy," Barrington was cautioning. "Set your spurs high and coast. It doesn't cost anything."

Grey made no reply. What difference did it make?

Then he had eased himself aboard, was settling in the saddle. How he hated the crowd out there! It meant nothing to them that he was risking his life just for their entertainment.

"Let me have him!"

Barrington himself whipped off the blind. A cowboy dropped the gate-poles. The outlaw lunged across the corral towards freedom, hit the hard-packed ground with a force that drove the breath from Grey's body.

The brute was outside, had swapped ends, was sun-fishing away from the cheering crowd. For all Grey could do, its terrific lunges were popping his bones, rattling his teeth. Blood was pounding in his ears. Pains stabbed his head.

Still he disregarded Barrington's suggestion, was not coasting. He was raking the outlaw from shoulder to rump, tearing great tufts of hair each time his spurs struck.

Now Widow-Maker was up where he could look down on the open-mouthed crowd. Now he was down where he could almost touch the ground with his whipping arm. The cheers had

ceased. The onlookers watched, tense, motionless.

The brute was heading for the home pasture,
bawling as it went. Grey's breath came in
laboured gasps. Sweat was streaming from his
body. Through hazy eyes he caught the face of
Judy, stark white in the morning sun. She was
still stifling her cries with a handkerchief.
Barrington stood beside her, one arm thrown
carelessly across her shoulder. It angered Grey
beyond reason. Why, he didn't know.

He got a glimpse of Alice. For all its usual
whiteness, her face now was flushed. After all,
she was proving herself a good sport.

Widow-Maker sun-fished, was going away
again in a belly-swelling lunge. Grey dared a
look back. The effort destroyed his balance. He
was slipping. The bone-crushing plunges were
too much for him.

He fought gamely for equilibrium. He was
canting far to the left. Again, as at Arapahoe, the
brute had broken his knee-grip. Only seconds
would elapse before he left the saddle. He
found himself looking for a soft place to land.
He didn't care. The reward for riding the brute
was a thousand dollars. And Alice had
promised . . .

"Ride that bronc or I'll slap your face," Judy
had said.

He managed to jerk straight in the saddle.

Widow-Maker was heading across the yard, pitching as he ran, hind legs of rubber, bull-frogged, front legs stiff as pistons. Each time he hit the ground it kinked Grey's aching neck. But he had regained his balance and was rowelling the outlaw from shoulder to rump. Once, as Widow-Maker sun-fished, he had a chance at an eye. His booted foot slung forward. A gouge of the spur-rowel and Widow-Maker would quit, blinded, defeated for ever. But he couldn't bring himself to do it.

The brute changed its course, headed directly for the pasture fence. Grey shuddered. He had seen a rider down in wire, would never forget the ripping, slashing of the knife-like barbs. But his bet was he could ride the outlaw to a finish. He stuck grimly.

Of a sudden he knew he had won. The horse had slowed down. Its plunges lacked steam. For all their tiredness, Grey's knees tightened. From somewhere back there he could hear Harmon shouting. The crowd was screaming. Above the confusion he caught the voice of Judy.

"You've got him whipped," she was crying shrilly. "Buck that bronc, or kill him, cowboy!"

Judy! Only she could have said such a thing; only a rider who had been up on a bucking horse could sense the sudden turn towards victory. He wondered how Judy rode. He knew he would be fearful if he ever saw her astride a pitching horse. But he also knew she would win as he was winning on Widow-Maker.

Again, as at Arapahoe, success was within his grasp. Directly ahead loomed the barbed-wire fence. Other horses would have veered off. But the jughead beneath him . . .

His spurs were lacing blood from the fury-blinded brute's sides. He whipped off his hat, fell to beating it alongside the head. Widow-Maker clung to his course.

They were in the barbed wire. The outlaw hit it sidewise, went to its knees. Two strands snapped . . . a third and fourth held. Grey could hear the treacherous strands singing about him. He saw blood—red blood spurting from the shoulder of the outlaw. His leather chaps, boot tops had saved his own legs. But they were badly ripped. The horse was struggling to rise. Still the strands were hissing and spitting. He tried to kick loose from the stirrups. The foot nearest the fence was caught.

Grey closed his eyes. This was the end. What did it matter? He loved Judy; his heart was calling to her. But he couldn't have her. She was married to Barrington. The face of Alice came to him. Stark terror was in her widened eyes, terror for his safety.

The horse beneath him was hopelessly tangled, might at any second go over on its side.

To stay with the wildly floundering animal meant death or injury.

He managed to kick loose from the stirrups, quit the brute in a flying leap. He landed sprawling. A great cry beat on his ears. The moment his weight left the saddle Widow-Maker was up. But the brute made no attempt to run. It stood cowed, quivering, blood streaming from ugly gashes in its shoulder.

Grey got slowly to his feet. Then he was lurching back towards the corral. The cheering crowd ran out to greet him. In the lead was Judy. She rushed forward to seize his hand.

"I'm proud of you, cowboy," she cried brokenly. "You're the greatest rider I ever saw. Grey . . ." She drew back quickly, flushed, ". . . please . . . not here."

Stunned by the terrific punishment he had endured, he had reached out for her. She had pulled away with the whispered supplication. It brought him back to his senses. He squared himself, walked past her. Alice was in his arms.

"Grey," she choked. "You did it, Grey. You won!"

He patted her shoulder solicitously, pushed her aside. He was face to face with Harmon. Still on beyond was Barrington—Barrington, who was watching him strangely.

"Had to quit him, huh?" Harmon bawled. "Can't take it!"

"What the hell are you talking about?" Grey

flung back. "I stayed with the brute even after he hit the fence. Is it in your rules that a man has to get ripped to pieces with barbed wire?"

"You made a good ride, cowboy," Barrington said in a dead voice. He shrugged, turned away.

"Where's my thousand?" Grey demanded, furious at Harmon, nettled by Barrington's strange attitude. Perhaps big Hugh had noticed Judy run out to meet him, noticed that before he thought he had attempted to draw her into his arms. "I rode that horse."

"The hell you did," Harmon shouted. "The rules were—"

"You'll get your thousand, Grey." It was Alice at his elbow. "Come to the office to-night. You were marvellous. You'll get your thousand or . . ." Harmon whirled and strode away towards the house.

Chapter XII

Grey Sage never forgot that night on the Cross Anchor. It changed the course of his life, plunged him into a mad whirl of events that found him a helpless victim.

He had dinner with Alice at a small table in a corner of the big dining-room. When they had finished, the girl left him. At her insistence—she seemed determined to let nothing stand between them—Grey, too, left the table presently and made his way to the room that served as the office of the big dude ranch. The sound of voices halted him just outside. He paused, not so much to overhear—although he recognized the voices as those of Alice and Harmon—as to cool the anger still smouldering within him. Harmon's attitude at the corrals had been the last straw. Alice's show of authority, together with her open avowal of love, had him bewildered. Of only one thing was he sure. He was determined not to marry Alice until he had succeeded in overcoming the fear he had of her.

Knowledge that in spite of this fear he cared for her deeply had come to him during the meal they had eaten in silence. He cared for her as a man would care for a delicate flower—a thing he must protect always, lest it be bruised and broken.

"There is no use in haggling, Uncle John," Alice's voice came to him clearly as he stood at the door. "My mind is made up. Even you cannot expect a man to stay on a horse and be cut to pieces in barbed wire. Grey rode that horse."

"He didn't," Harmon shouted angrily. "Besides, look at the horse. Ripped from hell to breakfast. It will be weeks before I can buck him. And him the topnotcher in my string. It means a cancellation of my contracts. The loss in money alone, to say nothing of the prestige of the Harmon wild string, will run into thousands."

"I'm not interested in that either," Alice's voice came chillingly. "I begged you not to do this. But you would attempt to prove that Grey couldn't ride that horse you prize so highly. He did. At least, as far as I am concerned—and as far as every one else on the ranch is concerned. If you want to make an issue of it, and filch out on the wager, you'll lose half of our guests. Grey Sage is a hero here. My advice is to consider carefully any move you make."

"I won't pay," Harmon thundered. "The rules were—"

"You admitted before every one there were no rules," the girl reminded coldly. "You will pay or else—"

"Or else what?"

Conscious of ears that burned at eavesdropping. Grey waited her explanation, as he could almost picture Harmon waiting.

"Or else I'll take over the Cross Anchor!" Her tone was determined.

"You take over the ranch!" Harmon broke into loud laughter. But it did not ring true. "You couldn't run it. You don't know the first thing about it. You'd go broke in a year, a quarter-of-a-million-dollar investment wiped out."

"Perhaps I couldn't run it alone," Alice countered in the smooth, cool voice that so terrified Grey, "but there are others who could."

"Barrington, I suppose? Well, don't count on him. I've taken all the lip I'm going to from that jasper. I'm firing him to-night. With him gone, just who do you think would take over here?"

"What's the matter with Grey Sage?"

The cowboy outside started.

Again Harmon laughed—sardonically, Grey thought. Anyway, it increased his smoking fury.

"That walloper couldn't run anything. What is he? Just a cowhand with a lucky break. This winning streak will blow up. Then watch him. Why, he can't—"

"That's enough," Alice cut in. "You're talking about the man I am going to marry."

"Marry!" Harmon's voice was a hoarse whisper. "Have you lost your mind? It wouldn't last two weeks. Imagine you married to a penniless cowboy who isn't fitted to do anything, who couldn't even meet your friends. You, worth a million in your own right, educated, refined. You're crazy. I won't stand for it."

"I am going to marry Grey Sage, and I don't know how you can stop me. On this wager you'll either listen to reason or I'll take over the management of the ranch myself. As for Barrington—go ahead and let him go, run him clear out of the country if you want to."

"Certainly you want Barrington to go," Harmon said maliciously. "No need for me to ask why."

"Why?" There was no question in the suddenly small voice of the girl.

"Because Grey Sage is in love with his wife, that's why. You know it; everybody knows it around here except that big-mouthed drunk, Barrington himself."

"You have no right to say that. Grey loves me. It's me he is going to marry." Her voice dropped until it chilled the cowboy with its coldness. "If you ever say anything like that again. I'll—I'll . . . I've stood for your brutality long enough. You've made your threats . . . treated the men and guests like dogs . . . deliberately tried to have trouble with Grey. You're paying that wager and you're getting out. I'll attend to things around here myself from now on. I'll have the books audited."

"You'll do nothing of the sort," he shouted. Grey heard him come to his feet, leap across the room. "I'll kill that damned drifter before you marry him."

A stifled sob from the girl galvanized Grey to action. All the fighting blood within him surged to his head. His eyes looked and saw red. He would marry Alice now, if for no other reason than to show Harmon that threats would avail him nothing. He would break him as he had broken Widow-Maker.

As the wild resolve possessed him, he found himself casting about for some excuse, any excuse to still his protesting conscience. Somewhere there must be a reason for this marriage beside revenge. There was Judy! He must protect her. It was the way out to silence the wagging tongues from which Harmon apparently had his information. That would set at rest the rumours, the innuendos, the whispered slurs of the old ladies in the rocking-chairs on the veranda. He'd marry Alice if it was the last thing he ever did. His fear of her . . . why should he fear a slip of a girl?

All the things that had piled up in his mind in the past weeks—since that day he had left the homestead and launched out for himself—suddenly centred in one moment that found him utterly alone. Before, he had taken his troubles to Mason. Now there was no one, no living soul in whom he could confide. That is, no one but Judy. If he could see her, she would understand. Wise had been the counsel of old Mason. He longed for it now. The cowman's warning was ringing in his ears.

"Don't marry an Eastern girl . . . marry a girl of the West. . . ."

Grey groaned inwardly, started away. He couldn't go through with it.

A stifled scream from Alice. He turned the knob, hurled open the door, leaped inside. The scene that met his eyes blinded him with rage. Harmon had seized hold of the girl, was choking her. Already she was limp, wilting in his hands, his fury beyond all sense or reason.

In a half-dozen great bounds, Grey Sage was beside them. He clapped a hand on Harmon's shoulder, jerked him round. The big fellow let go of the girl with an oath. The furious blow he unloosed whistled by Grey's ears. The cowboy ducked. His first thought was of Alice. She had fallen in a chair, slumped over, with her head cushioned in arms outflung across a table. She was gasping for breath. Great red bruises marked her throat. But apparently she was more shocked and frightened than hurt.

He started towards her. But Harmon was after him, cursing under his breath, his weather-pitted face purple with apoplectic fury. Grey side-stepped. His fists balled. A slashing right brought blood spurting from Harmon's nose. Still the big fellow came on.

Save for what he had learned in a few rough-and-tumble fights, Grey knew nothing of self-defence. But his was a fighting heart. Yet in Harmon he recognized a man who had been trained scientifically. He could tell by the way the blows were timed, the way they were now smashing him at will. They stung terribly. He was being beaten back, smothered under a fusillade of blows.

For the moment his confidence deserted him. He hated himself for that instant of weakness. He had known it twice before—aboard Widow-Maker. Now here he was in his third big battle— and showing yellow.

From the corner of his eye he caught a movement by Alice. She had raised up, was watching them with terrified eyes. She sprang to her feet, hands clutching her bruised throat.

"Don't, Grey," she pleaded. "Please . . for my sake. He's an old man. He's no match for you."

"No match for him," Harmon roared. "I'll beat him to death. The damned drifter!"

Cornered, Grey Sage lashed out wildly. His fist found the other's chin, silenced his bellowed threats. From outside came a burst of laughter . . . the guests still lingering over their dinner, the sounds of the fight drowned by their conversation.

"Uncle John!" It was Alice pleading shrilly. "I'm through with the ranch. Take it; all I want is—"

What she was about to say was never finished. At that moment Harmon made a terrific swing. His fist struck Grey a glancing blow, set his ear to burning. Harmon spun round, off balance. Grey put everything he had behind a right. It came whistling in, struck solidly at the base of Harmon's ear. With a hollow grunt the big fellow lurched backwards, came up against the wall, pitched headlong to the floor.

Alice was in Grey's arms, a frightened, white-faced creature clinging desperately. The panting cowboy drew her to him, while he wiped the streaming sweat from his brow.

"Get your duds," he said in a tone the strength of which amazed even himself. "We're going to town."

"Town . . . what for? . . . Uncle John . . ."

"To hell with Uncle John!" he rasped out. She pulled away from him to stare. "We're going to be married to-night."

"Grey!" She was back in his arms.

He folded her close, strong now in his victory. It was the age-old battle he had fought—a man's battle for a woman. And that woman in his arms. At the moment he only knew that he had won her in combat, that she was his, was alluringly sweet, terrified half out of her senses.

Harmon was sitting up, muttering, rubbing his jaw. Through glazed eyes he saw them, tried to rise. He only succeeded in staggering to his feet, slumping into a chair at the table. Alice went over to him.

Grey strode outside.

"I'm sorry," Grey heard her say. "But you—"

"Get the hell out of here!" Harmon snarled. "You haven't heard the last of me. I'm through. I'm cleaning up the affairs of the ranch. From this night on you run it."

"I know you are. Grey Sage—my husband—is the new manager of the Cross Anchor."

Harmon's answer was lost to Grey as he stamped down the hallway and out on the veranda.

Chapter XIII

Alice Harmon and Grey Sage were married that night in Arapahoe. Behind the wheel of her expensive roadster Alice had burned up the road from the Cross Anchor, the cowboy sitting in glum silence beside her. Now that he had time to think, he couldn't find coherency, any more than he had been able to in other times of stress. He hated himself for that apparent weakness, of never being able to face an obstacle and overcome it at the moment, for always waiting until the thing was past to work out a solution.

Once they were on the road in the moonlight he forgot everything, and was conscious only of the girl. From time to time he stole glances at her—glances of inquiry, as though he wondered who this strange and beautiful creature was with whom he was racing through the night. Even in the wan light he could see the bruises on her throat. They stood out with terrifying clearness against her dead-white skin.

"Will you always love me, Grey?" she whispered, one hand finding his to grip his fingers.

"Yes," he muttered. Not because he meant it, but because he could think of no other answer at the moment.

Then they were in the outskirts of the city. She slowed down. It was late. There was a feeling of unfriendliness along the darkened streets. The yawning alleyways were cold, forbidding.

"How are we going to arrange this thing?" Alice was asking in a low voice. "After all, I don't elope every day in the year . . . with an infuriated uncle cursing my wedding plans. Do you know what we have to do?"

"Just get married." He tried to grin, but the effort was a failure. "Mebbeso we'd better rout out Brown, the rodeo secretary. He's married . . . he'll probably be able to tell us what to do."

"Why didn't we bring Hugh and Judy? They could have told us exactly how it is done. They eloped, you know, just like this."

Hugh and Judy! He could scarcely stifle the groan that rose up within him. Glad indeed he was that Judy had not come along. He could not have gone through with the thing. One look from Judy and he . . . but that was past now. No longer would he think of her. She was the wife of another man. Her protection from the innuendos was partly behind his mad resolve to marry Alice.

He looked again at the girl. He wondered why he didn't care for her as he cared for Judy. She was so alluringly lovely—a marble waif in the moonlight—possessed of an austere beauty that could thrill any man. And she was his . . . would soon be his wife. The thought did not elate him. Rather it left him dead, hating himself.

With some difficulty they located the home of

Tom Brown. Feeling strangely ill at ease, Grey crawled out of the car, strode up on the porch and rang the bell. Presently a light flashed on . . . soft footsteps were coming towards the door. The sudden blinding glare of an incandescent globe above startled him.

Recognizing him, Brown threw open the door.

"For Pete's sake, what are you doing here at this time of night, Sage?" he demanded, pumping the cowboy's hand.

"Getting married." Grey attempted without success to swallow his embarrassment. "Wondered if you'd show me how."

"Getting married! Who's the lucky lady? Do we know her?"

"Unlucky, you mean," Grey corrected nervously. "It's Alice Harmon."

"Alice Harmon?" Brown pulled him into the hallway. "You lucky devil! Now, I suppose, we'll lose the best bronc-rider in the game. Where's the bride-to-be?"

"Out in front in her car. Fact is, it's a sort of an elopement. We figured—"

"Quit figuring," Brown said. "When a man gets a girl like Alice this far along towards the altar, he's done all that is to be expected of him." He stepped on the porch. "Miss Harmon," he called, "shut off the motor and come on in. I'll arrange everything from here. I'll have the missus up in a jiffy."

He dashed back in the house. Grey heard him

shouting excitedly for his wife. He went back to the curb and helped Alice from the car. She stepped beside him, gave him one of those inscrutable glances that so many times had caused him to wonder.

"Are you sure of yourself?" she asked.

"Yes." But he did not meet her gaze squarely. With an attempt at a gay laugh, he grasped her arm. Together they went up to the porch.

Mrs. Brown was coming towards them, pulling on a negligee over a nightgown. Brown was directly behind. He had slipped on his clothes, was trying to smooth his rumpled hair.

"Alice Harmon!" Mrs. Brown was greeting the girl gushingly. "Isn't this glorious? We're glad you came here. Now, Tom, get right on that telephone. You have to rouse the county clerk and get a marriage licence . . . unless you folks have one. Have you?"

"Didn't know you needed one," Grey admitted frankly.

"Certainly you do." Alice smiled. "I don't believe you ever have been married before."

"Have you?" he demanded.

"Well, not exactly."

He wondered what she meant. But he had no time to ponder it. Brown was on the 'phone. And Mrs. Brown had piloted them into the living-room, was pottering about solicitously, trying to make them feel at ease.

"We've got to go to the county clerk's office," Brown said presently. "He'll meet us there. The justice of the peace will be here when we get back. The missus and I will stand up with you. And we might pick up a ring or something—"

"Never mind the ring," Alice put in. "I've got so many now I haven't fingers enough for them."

Grey looked at her strangely. That remark, and the one she had made about not exactly having been married worried him, a sort of a vague torment that persisted. Brown's next question drove home to him further the gulf that lay between them.

"Go in your car or mine?"

"Take mine," Alice answered. "I'll make myself presentable while you're gone. Here are the keys, Grey."

"But . . ." Grey flushed. ". . . I can't drive."

Alice regarded him in utter amazement.

"My, how your education has been neglected! Here, Mr. Brown, you drive my car. But be careful you don't drive too fast for Grey. He might get carsick. It isn't a bronc, you know."

Grey spun about to hide the sudden paleness that had driven the colour from his cheeks. For the moment he was tempted to dash out, leave Alice for ever.

"Let's get going," Brown said, conscious of the sudden tenseness.

Together the two men left the house. Brown slid

in under the wheel of Alice's roadster. In silence Grey crawled in beside him. Nor did he speak until they arrived at the courthouse to find the shivering county clerk waiting. He replied grumpily to their questions, plainly none too well pleased at being routed out of bed for a licence.

Presently, however, they had it, and were roaring back towards the house.

They found the justice of the peace already arrived. Alice, more coldly beautiful than ever, had taken time to tidy up a bit—although if she ever was anything but immaculate, Grey had not noticed. And now she was far more composed than he. For all his attempts to appear natural, his nerves were jumping. She came over to him, slipped an arm through his.

"You're nervous," she accused. "So am I . . . just a little."

Still he said nothing. His lips had taken on the grim set that thousands had seen when he came out aboard a bronc at the rodeo.

The ceremony was brief. The Browns stood up with them. Almost before Grey realized it, the justice of the peace was propounding the old question:

"Do you, Grey Sage, take this woman to be your lawfully wedded wife . . . for better or for worse . . . until death do you part?"

"I do." His voice was strong, vibrant with a strident note.

Alice was saying: "I do." Her tone was low, scarcely audible. She was looking straight ahead. And he thought he saw a tear glisten on her lashes. He wondered. . . .

The justice had closed his little manual, was shaking hands with him. Brown had kissed Alice. Then she stood alone before Grey. He looked at her for a moment, a half-fearful light in his eyes. He started to turn away.

"It's the custom for a new husband to kiss his bride," the justice reminded beamingly.

"Yes, start the thing off right with a kiss," Mrs. Brown teased.

Awkwardly Grey took Alice in his arms. He trembled at her closeness. But even now he could not shake off the feeling that he had no right to touch her, that she was only a beautifully chiselled stone.

"You needn't bother if it hurts you," she whispered. "I didn't realize." She was dangerously near tears.

"Didn't realize what?" he asked in a low tone.

"That you . . . felt like this . . . hated me. I thought—"

"I don't hate you."

He tilted up her head, kissed her. Her lips were cold. But he tingled under the contact. She lay in his arms—a limp and languid gesture that made him feel she was only enduring this caress. If the Browns noticed, they covered it neatly by their animated conversation.

Alice drew herself away.

"Don't make a show of the thing," she said in a tone that stung him deeply. "After all, there'll be endless years for mushing if . . . we feel like it." She left him abruptly, crossed the room.

He stood looking after her, scarcely knowing what to do, what to say.

Again the Browns took command of the embarrassing moment. Tom seized Grey by the arm to pilot him to the kitchen, where he mixed a drink. Mrs. Brown was already planning a round of parties and showers for the bride. But Alice plainly was not thrilled by the suggestion. She appeared suddenly tired. However, they could not escape before Mrs. Brown had prepared and served some refreshments.

Hours later it seemed they were in the roadster and headed back to the Cross Anchor. By now the moon hung low on the horizon, its glow ghostly in the Stygian void. The beam of their headlights pierced the darkness to reveal in the road deep and awesome cañons that did not exist, but which kept Alice constantly footing the brake.

"You might at least say something," she offered after a time.

"There isn't much to say, is there?"

He tried to make his reply careless. But he

failed. There was much to say. He just couldn't find words for it all. To himself there was this to say—for all old Mason's advice he had done exactly as he had been warned not to. He had married a girl of the East—a girl of wealth. He knew in his heart he could never bridge the gulf that lay between them. He felt that she, too, realized it—now, when it was too late.

"There is something that has been bothering me," he said.

"Yes?"

She did not take her eyes from the road. He could not help but thrill to the picture she made as she bent over the wheel.

"That remark of yours about not having been married. You said you never had been married—exactly."

She threw back her head and laughed.

"Jealous?" she taunted. "Well, that's some consolation, anyway. I'd rather have you jealous than just lukewarm. As long as you have given it a thought, just worry along with it for a time. I'll tell you someday. At least it will make you consider me occasionally."

"I've thought of you since the moment I first laid eyes on you, but I'm—I'm—"

"You're what?" She took her foot from the accelerator, half turned, her features shadowed in the dim glow of the dash light.

"I'm afraid of you," he blurted out.

"Still afraid of me? Why?"

"Because you're so lovely, I guess . . . because you're so different . . . so rich . . . well, just because."

She slipped the gears and jerked the emergency brake, bringing the car to a halt. She edged out from under the wheel and over against him. Suddenly her arms were round his neck, her body pressed close to him. He could feel her pounding heart. Her lips were just below his— enticing red lips.

He was crushing her brutally, paying no heed to her gasping breath, her little cries under the pressure of his strong arms. She tried to speak. His lips had found hers. Unspeakable pleasure, almost pain, possessed him. After all, he did love Alice. She was his. This charming creature was his wife.

"You don't ever need to be afraid of me," she was gasping as she pulled her lips away. "And you don't need to be so rough, either. I hate to be mussed up."

Her words sent his arms down. Again the barrier reared up between them, stark, sinister. Again she gave him that strange inscrutable look.

"A woman doesn't always mean what she says," she pouted, sliding back under the wheel. The motor snarled, the car shot ahead. "Women like to be shown. Sometimes they might even want to be . . . beaten down."

The grim whiteness of his lips, visible even in the gloom, halted her. She knew that again, as at Brown's, she had wounded his outer sensitiveness. With reckless speed she sent the car roaring ahead through the night.

No word passed between them. At the ranch she nosed the roadster into the garage, snapped off the ignition. For a moment she sat looking at him. He only regarded her in silence. She leaped from the car, slammed the door. He followed her, deeply conscious now of the embarrassing silence, yet seemingly incapable of breaking it.

At the porch she paused.

"You're coming in?" There was a sudden shyness in her voice.

"No. I'll go on down to the bunkhouse."

"You mean . . . you're going to your own . . ."

"Yes."

She sprang up the steps and ran into the house. He strode away without a backward look. His mind was in a whirl. He hated himself for his coldness. Yet he hadn't meant to be cold. He scarcely knew what he did mean. For in the long silence his fear of the girl had increased. He felt himself inferior. Other men—men of her own class—could have coped with the situation. But he . . . his only defence had been in silence . . . silence in the presence of . . . his wife.

Chapter XIV

Grey Sage never reached the bunkhouse at the Cross Anchor ranch that night of his wedding to Alice Harmon. Before he had taken a dozen steps a scream brought him about.

"Grey! Grey!" It was Alice crying hysterically. "Uncle John . . . Grey, he's . . ."

He bounded back to join her on the veranda. Behind her grouped the guests, talking excitedly in hushed tones. He seized hold of Alice's arm, attempted to draw her into the shadows of the porch.

"Take it easy, now," he cautioned. "What is it?"

Before he asked, he knew. He could tell by the way she was clinging to him. There was only one thing that could cause such stark terror; only one thing that caused people to huddle about and talk in awesome whispers.

"Uncle John is dead," she choked. "Oh, Grey, they found him in his office . . . in the chair where we last saw him."

For all his efforts to pilot her across the veranda, she had turned and was pushing through the staring group, pulling him inside. They gained the door of the office, opened it quietly, entered. John Harmon sat where he had slumped down after the fight. His head lay across outflung arms on the desk. Apparently, in the several hours they had been gone, he had made no move.

"Did any one think of the coroner?" Grey asked, going outside to face the crowd, which had followed to gather about curiously.

"Yes . . . and the sheriff," someone answered.

"The sheriff?"

"You were overheard having an argument with Harmon . . ."

Grey did not wait for the fellow to finish. He went back into the office, closed the door behind him. "Where's Barrington?" he demanded of Alice.

"I don't know. No one seems to have seen him."

"There's nothing you can do here. Go to your room and rest for a time. I'll hunt Hugh. When the coroner comes, I'll call you." He lifted her face and kissed her tenderly—the first kiss that had meant anything, he thought. But this one did. And she responded to it, her cheeks wet with tears, her lips moist, eager.

"I want to be with you, Grey," she said.

"All right. Come on."

He strode through the guests, who parted for them, only to gather again in knots.

Barrington and Judy they located some time later at the far end of the big dining-room, talking. The two rose as they approached. With only a word of greeting to Alice, Judy came directly to Grey.

"You keep a stiff upper lip, cowboy." Her voice was low, tremulous. "We're with you."

Before Grey could reply, Barrington had taken him by the arm.

"Too bad," he consoled. "But, then, it might have happened to any one. If you've got anything on your chest you want to get off, spill it."

"Anything on my chest?" Grey repeated, dumbfounded. "What are you talking about?"

Barrington looked at him strangely.

"Only what a couple of the guests said—a couple of the old women. They were passing the office . . . claim they heard you and Harmon having an argument. They say they distinctly heard someone threaten to kill someone else. You were in there with Harmon." Not until then did the full import of the gossip strike Grey. So that was it? They were trying to implicate him in Harmon's death.

"We did have a row," he admitted. "But I didn't . . . it was heart failure."

"I'm not so sure," Barrington said.

"What do you mean?" Grey demanded.

"Just what I said . . . I'm not sure John Harmon wasn't murdered."

"But there must be some reason for you thinking that?" Alice put in quickly.

Barrington had turned away at the sudden arrival of a group of men. They were moving directly towards them.

"Howdy, Barrington . . . sorry to intrude this way, Miss Harmon," one, a hawk-faced man of ministerial bearing, said courteously. "I'm Merton Crawley, the coroner. Your uncle is . . .."

"Right there in the office." Grey spoke for Alice. "These other gentlemen?"

"Summers, the sheriff," Barrington said, indicating a beefy fellow with a florid face and a gaudy cowhide vest on which glinted a star, "and Dr. Barnett."

The latter bowed in an elegant manner—a manner which seemed to fit perfectly with his slight build, his sleek appearance.

Then the three officials were moving towards the office. Alice, Judy, Barrington and Grey followed. At the door, Grey turned.

"You girls had better stay outside. You've had enough for one night. We'll keep you posted."

Alice and Judy left. Grey stepped inside to watch with horrible fascination as the doctor started about his examination in a methodical, disinterested manner. Barrington, too, stood by—nervously, Grey thought. But he did not blame the big foreman for that. The ordeal was enough to tighten the strongest nerves.

Presently the sheriff left, pausing to ask a few questions of Grey. The cowboy replied in monosyllables.

After a cursory inspection the doctor straightened up. He spoke in an undertone to the coroner.

"Call Sheriff Summers," he ordered Grey.

Glad of the opportunity to be away, Grey went

outside to locate the sheriff. He found him drinking with a group of guests. He returned with him to the office.

Once there, the coroner drew the officer aside. Together with the doctor they held a hurried conference. When they had concluded, the sheriff came over to plant himself before Grey, tuck his thumbs into the armpits of his cowhide vest and pin him with a sharp scrutiny, the while he rolled a cigar in his lips.

"You had an argument with Harmon to-night?" he announced rather than asked. "There were threats?"

"On his part, yes," Grey replied.

"There was a fight . . . the doctor says there are bruises on Harmon's face and body."

"We had a fight."

"That being the case, there is nothing for me to do but arrest you."

"What for?"

"For the murder of John Harmon."

"But Harmon wasn't murdered. He died of apoplexy."

"How do you know?" the sheriff shot in, none too friendly.

"I don't. I just thought—"

"Well, you thought wrong. John Harmon was murdered. You are held for the coroner's jury. The inquest will be to-morrow."

"John Harmon murdered! An inquest!" Still

the full meaning of the thing did not dawn upon Grey Sage. "Me held for . . . why, I wasn't even here when this happened."

"An alibi is easily proved if you have one," the sheriff grunted. "Meanwhile, you're coming along with me."

"All right." There was nothing else for Grey to say. "May I speak to my wife before I go?"

"Your wife?" Barrington said quickly. "You mean—"

"Alice and I were married in Arapahoe to-night."

"Go ahead," the sheriff granted before Barrington could express his surprise. "I'll give you ten minutes. But don't try to break for it."

Grey strode away. He found Alice and Judy together in the former's room. He rapped timidly.

Alice threw open the door.

"What is it?" There was deep anxiety in her voice.

"I'm under arrest," he said grimly.

"You . . . under . . . arrest? What . . . for?"

"For the murder of your uncle."

"Uncle John murdered?"

A stifled scream burst from her. She would have fallen had he not reached out quickly and caught her. Judy, too, sprang over beside him. For a moment their gazes met. There was pain in Judy's eyes—pain and hurt too deep to hide. He knew without asking that Alice had told her— knew that it was not this grim tragedy which had descended upon the Cross Anchor that was uppermost in her mind, but his marriage.

"You know, then?" he asked in a low voice.

"Yes." She could scarcely get out the word. "And I want to . . . congratulate you." She turned away, lips tight-pressed, fled from the room.

Lifting Alice in his arms, Grey laid her on a couch. He knelt down beside her, smoothed the black hair back from her forehead. It was the first time he had touched her thus. Her skin was smooth as velvet under his rough and awkward hand.

"They arrested you," she murmured brokenly. "Oh, Grey, and on our wedding night. It seems as though—"

"I'll come through all right," he told her without assurance. "I'll just be going along now with the sheriff."

"You will not." She started up, clinging to him. "There must be some way. You're not going to jail. They have bond."

"Never mind the bond." His tone was suddenly tired. "I'll take the rap. I don't care much."

"Don't care? How can you say such a thing?"

"I don't know." He kissed her on the forehead, turned abruptly and left her.

Outside he rejoined the waiting sheriff. With the doctor and coroner he left the Cross Anchor ranch house, climbed wearily in their car and was again streaking back through the night towards Arapahoe.

Chapter XV

The inquest into the death of John Harmon brought out some startling facts—facts that dumbfounded the guests of the Cross Anchor and staggered Grey Sage, who speedily became enmeshed in a web of circumstantial evidence from which there seemed no escape.

John Harmon was murdered! The coroner and doctor testified to it. He had been struck on the back of the head with a blunt instrument that had shattered his skull.

Witness followed witness in quick succession. Two guests of the ranch, Mrs. Erick Van Ressalder of New York and her scandal-mongering companion, Mrs. Worthington Truebolt of Philadelphia —from whose whispered innuendos Grey had tried to shield Judy—testified to having heard a quarrel. They both swore they had recognized the voices of Grey Sage and John Harmon raised in anger.

When Grey took the stand he made no attempt to deny the damning testimony. He merely attempted to establish an alibi. He swore that Harmon had not been dead when he had left the ranch. Further than that he refused to talk. For suddenly it came to him that he had left that room before Alice, left her with the living Harmon. The thought sealed his lips. Anything he said might implicate her—a thing he resolved not to do whatever the cost.

After a seemingly interminable period of questioning, which left him trembling and strangely fearful, the jury filed out. He sat gripping the arms of his chair with bloodless hands. Alice looked at him beseechingly. She was trying to cheer him, but cheering him was out of the question.

He tried not to look at Judy. The vagrant glances that did stray in her direction revealed that she was struggling to hold back tears. Big Hugh, beside her, patted her arm, a gesture that annoyed Grey.

The fact that he and Alice were married was brought out on the stand. The news set up a buzz of comment among the guests from the Cross Anchor, who had come in a body. Grey paid no heed. What did he care for them—for any one, for that matter? He saw them now through eyes that had grown suspicious—eyes which looked out upon the whole crowd as unfriendly, willing at the first opportunity to crucify him.

The jury filed in. The long faces filled Grey with apprehension. With heartbreaking slowness they seated themselves. The sound of their movements crashed down on taut nerves. The foreman rose, adjusted gold-rimmed spectacles on a thin nose. His faltering words rang like a tocsin in Grey's ears.

"We, the jury, find that John Harmon came to his death as the result of blows on the head administered by a person or persons unknown . . . and recommend that Grey Sage be remanded to the district court for trial on charges of murder."

The nervous foreman sat down, still trying, without success, to adjust the gold-rimmed spectacles on his quivering nose.

Grey was conscious of the same sensation that shot through him aboard a bronc coming out of a chute. But then there was an outlet for his pent-up emotions. Now there was none—no recourse but to sit by dumbly and hear his doom pronounced.

The coroner was gathering up his notes. The doctor had ducked out quickly. The sheriff was coming towards him.

"You heard the verdict," he said. "Come along. I've got to lock you up."

Alice seized his arm.

"My lawyer is flying from New York. He'll be here in the morning. Meanwhile, can't bond be arranged?"

"There is no bond in a murder case in Wyoming," the sheriff announced importantly. "This cowboy will stay in jail until your lawyer figures some way to get him out on a technicality."

"He'll do that," Alice smiled wanly. "There are ways, you know."

"I'm just doing my duty, Miss Harmon," the sheriff muttered apologetically. "I didn't mean anything."

She slipped an arm through Grey's.

"We all know you didn't do this thing," she said. "We have faith in you. How they can even hold you is more than I can understand."

"But they have," Grey shrugged. His tone, the lifelessness of it, struck a chill within her.

"You won't be held long," she assured him. "I wired our family lawyer, Jay Mortimer. He's flying out. We'll have you back on the ranch soon."

"I don't want to come out until they have proved I didn't do it," Grey said stubbornly.

"You can't stay in jail," Alice cried.

"Other suspects do. I wouldn't consider being turned loose with this taint against my name. They'll find out I didn't do it."

"But what if they decide you did?"

"They can't prove any such thing. Justice can't be that crooked."

"We're not risking it."

"What you're trying to say is you're not real sure I didn't do it," he rasped out, seizing hold of her.

"You're hurting my arm. I didn't say that. I merely said we were going to get you out of jail."

"And I'm saying I'm not leaving jail until they prove I did not commit this crime."

Their gazes locked. Hers was the first to fall. What she saw convinced her that Grey Sage meant exactly what he said.

"You're upset," she soothed. "Go on with the sheriff now. I'll see you in the morning. If there is anything you want, get word to me."

Grey scarcely noticed the kiss she pecked on his cheek as he turned to follow the sheriff from the room.

A night of sleepless tossing left him dishevelled, eyes bloodshot, nerves frayed. His predicament was too weirdly improbable for reason, a fitting climax to the sudden and bewildering changes that had crowded his life in a few weeks. His way had been pointed out clearly by old Mason. He belonged to the rodeos. He had deserted his career, had married an Eastern girl against the advice of the wise old cowhand.

And now, as though to show him the error of his ways, he was accused of murder. He could not understand the charge nor understand why, when he was telling the truth on oath, the coroner's jury didn't believe him. Once he thought perhaps the jury, composed of men from ordinary walks of life —some almost shabbily dressed—might have done the thing in spite against Alice, who had come to the coroner's office in rustling silks. She had swept in regally, a thing that even he noticed. In the short time he had followed the rodeo he had learned something of crowd psychology;

he knew how crowds hated affectation, how they could retaliate for snobbery or affront. This might possibly have been at the bottom of the verdict.

The murder? He could not bring himself to believe that Harmon really was murdered. But there had been the doctor's evidence. It stood out like a burning brand in his mind.

"John Harmon was killed with some blunt instrument . . . a fracture of the skull."

The doctor had refused to testify that the instrument had been the butt of a gun. He had persisted that it was a blunt instrument. Nor could deft and tricky questioning make him say otherwise. Beyond this point he had revealed nothing. Neither had other witnesses, particularly the loquacious Van Ressalder and Truebolt women, who prattled on despite frantic attempts to silence them. Sifted down, they had admitted nothing more than that they had heard an argument—a truth he did not deny.

He himself had revealed Harmon's threat to kill him before he would allow the marriage of Alice. He had bared his story in a straightforward manner, holding nothing back except the fact that he left the room before Alice, trusting to the truth to exonerate him. Now that he had time to think, he found the truth only implicated him deeper—implicated him so strongly that he had been held to the district court for murder.

Again and again he reviewed the events of the night before, from the moment he had stopped outside the door to overhear the argument between Alice and her uncle, until he had slammed away leaving Harmon panting in a chair from which, apparently, he never rose. He had left Alice in that room. But the idea of Alice killing her uncle was too ridiculous to consider. Yet, there had been no one else around: no one in the hallway when he had left. Of only one thing was he sure: he did not kill John Harmon. But who did? There his whirling mind always spun back again to start revolving in an endless chain.

He was making a brave attempt to eat the tasty breakfast the sheriff's wife had prepared for him when a key turned in the steel door.

"Right this way, Miss Harmon," he heard the sheriff's voice.

Grey dreaded the meeting with Alice, dreaded to have her see him in these surroundings. She had come of her own volition. There was nothing he could do about it now.

She came in swiftly, arms outstretched.

"You poor dear!" She kissed him in a motherly fashion. "How did you sleep?" He looked beyond her at a stranger—a tall, smartly dressed man of thirty-odd years with the face of a student. Shrewd, deep-set black eyes regarded him from beneath bushy eyebrows. A sleek pointed moustache jutted up towards high cheek-bones.

In a single glance Grey whipped him from his pearl-grey spats to the crown of a natty fedora.

"It's Jay, honey," Alice was saying—"Jay Mortimer, our New York lawyer. He's here to defend you."

"Glad to know you." Grey knew he lied. For he hated the man at a glance. There was something about the fellow that struck him as furtive, underhand. And Alice had stepped back beside him in a way Grey disliked.

The two men shook hands. The lawyer's grasp was firm and strong. Another time that grip, the steady black eyes that never left his face, might have inspired confidence within Grey.

"And now," Mortimer said in a business-like tone, "we've already started the ball rolling to have you released on bond. If that doesn't work, we'll get a habeas—"

"Don't trouble yourself," Grey cut in sourly. "I don't want out. I couldn't face folks with this hanging over me. I want to be cleared."

"Don't worry about that, old man," Mortimer slapped him on the back, a gesture that made Grey boil. "We'll fix everything."

"I don't want anything fixed." Grey was angered beyond reason by the fellow's brusque manner, his patronizing tone . . . angered at Alice . . . at every one. "I want it proved. Any lawyer nowadays can fix things. That doesn't help a man's conscience. I've been accused of a murder I didn't do. I want to be clear . . . want justice."

"I supposed you understood that was what I meant, my dear fellow," Mortimer said. "That's why I came: to clear you. Now we'll just run along, Alice, and see what can be done." He tucked her fingers under his arm.

"Don't put yourself to any trouble," Grey snorted, furious at this solicitous attitude towards Alice. "You might hurry up the trial if you can, but—"

"We've already attended to that. The fall term of the district court convenes next week. Your case will head the criminal docket. A very unusual proceeding . . . one mighty lucky for you."

"I don't want unusual proceedings," Grey shouted. "To hell with unusual proceedings! I'm innocent, I tell you. And I don't want money mixed up in it. A fellow who hasn't done anything doesn't have to buy himself a clear conscience."

The words struck him as odd—old Mason's philosophy on his own lips. But he had voiced the thing in his heart. He sensed that already the Harmon money had been set to work to ensure his release without definitely proving him innocent. And he was determined that he would accept no help from those millions.

"Quite right, quite right," Mortimer's words came to him. "And you can rest assured that we will exonerate you completely. Now we must be moving along. Come, my dear."

Grey Sage's fists balled. His first impulse was to strike down the fellow. He hung on to himself with an effort. Alice came forward, pecked his cheek with a dutiful kiss. He turned abruptly, strode across to the barred window. Alice, his bride, left the jail, clinging to the arm of the smartly garbed lawyer.

Chapter XVI

The days that passed were interminable to Grey Sage. He read, he slept, he paced, he stared out from the barred windows of the Arapahoe jail. He mulled over things in his mind until his head ached with the effort of thinking. He was not concerned with the outcome of the trial. In his innocence, he could conceive of no miscarriage of justice. It was the waiting that drove him to the point of madness—the constant arguing of Mortimer, who came daily to talk with him. He disliked the fellow more at each appearance. Sometimes it seemed that Mortimer was not satisfied in his own mind, was trying to get him to admit the murder. That only increased Grey's mounting hatred. He had one story. He repeated it until thought of it sickened him.

Alice, too, came daily to see him, always in company with Mortimer. Through the sheriff he learned that the lawyer was staying at the Cross Anchor and driving back and forth with the girl. Try as he would to convince himself that the thing meant nothing, that he did not care deeply enough for Alice to resent it, still there rankled in Grey's mind a thought that the woman he had married was glad of the opportunity to be with the smooth-talking Easterner.

Then one day there was a pleasant break in the deadly dullness of his incarceration. A timid voice came from the steel grating.

"Hello, cowboy."

He halted in his restless pacing.

Face plastered against the barred door was Judy Barrington. He bounded over to her, seized her hand.

"I'm glad you came," he cried happily, realizing that it was for this thing alone he had been waiting. He tried not to devour her with his eyes.

"How's the old spirit?" She made a poor attempt at gayness.

"Pretty good." He wondered why he always had to be so serious in the presence of this girl.

"Why didn't you get out on bond? Then we could have all planned your fight together, on the outside. As it is—"

"As it is . . . what?"

"Your friends haven't much to say about it." She refused to meet his gaze. "Mr. Mortimer and—"

"Judy," he used her given name with a naturalness that amazed him. If she even noticed she gave no sign. "Do you like this jasper, Mortimer?"

"I'd like to hamstring him," she said fiercely. "But, then, I haven't any right to say that. He's been perfectly lovely to me. And Alice is so worried. If it wasn't for him—"

It was on the tip of his tongue to ask her

about Alice and Mortimer. Pride held him silent. Instead, he reached out boldly and laid his hand on Judy's fingers that were gripping the steel bars.

"I'm glad you came," he said again. He tried not to accent the *you*.

"I'm glad . . . you're glad." Her eyes fell. She stood scuffing the bottom of the grating with the toe of a dainty slipper. "I've got to run along now. I'm expecting word from Hugh . . . and I may be leaving."

"Word from Hugh . . . leaving? What are you talking about?"

"Haven't you heard?" she asked in surprise. "I thought Alice would tell you. Hugh quit the ranch. He got wind of the fact somehow that Harmon had been ready to fire him with the consent of Alice. So he blew up and left. He's out signing contracts for his wild string. Going into the rodeo game in earnest. He's just as well off, I guess . . . happier, at least."

"Hugh left the ranch? Harmon did say he was going to let him go. That leaves Alice out there alone. Who's running the Cross Anchor?" There was real concern in his voice.

"Mr. Mortimer, I guess," Judy said with none too good grace. "He seems to be running every-thing."

"Damn Mortimer!" Grey blurted out. He started to pull away his hand—hardly conscious until now that he had been gripping her fingers. She clung to it.

"I know how you feel, cowboy," she whispered. "But keep a stiff upper lip. Things are bound to work out all right."

"You'll be here for the trial?" he demanded in a sudden panic, feeling strangely deserted and alone.

"Yes. Hugh has been subpoenaed as a material witness. He'll be back. I'll stay at the ranch until after the trial. Then . . ." Her voice trailed off wearily. "Oh, Grey, why did things have to be like this?"

"I don't know. And I haven't helped them any by blundering along, always getting my foot in it. But, Judy, no matter what happens, there's one thing I want you to know . . ."

"Sh-h-h!" She placed a finger on his lips. Before he thought he kissed it. She did not draw it away.

"I know what you are going to say. And I feel the same way, Grey. Perhaps some day there'll be a break for us. Until that time, what you were going to say goes for both of us."

"That makes me feel better. Half the misery of being in jail is the torment of not being able to see you occasionally, Judy. Is it so terribly wrong?"

"I don't know, Grey." Her voice was low, uncertain. "There might have been some way for us. Why didn't you tell me you were going to marry Alice?"

"I didn't know it myself. I'm still wondering how it came about. Can't you see . . . I . . . I don't know what I'm trying to say. Forget it."

She regarded him searchingly.

"You don't mean that, Grey. You don't mean you want me to forget it, do you?"

"Please don't," he whispered contritely. "Things have broken around me a little too fast. Seems like I can't think any more. I ought to have stayed on the homestead where I belonged." A deep stab of loneliness assailed him. How peaceful and quiet it was up there on the river now! How he had enjoyed the long rides, the hours of gazing out across the hazy flats to the blazing horizon! He had no worry there—just lazy, dreamy days of peace. "The trouble with me is I never know what I want until after it's too late to get it. Then I want it with all my heart, seems like I can't live without it."

"I guess all of us are like that—never knowing what we want, clutching at the first substitute for the real thing. We all pick phoneys, cowboy, all our lives. But why cry about it? If you can just pull through this, then perhaps we can begin again."

"If I can pull through?" he demanded. "Judy, you don't think I killed Harmon, do you?"

"I know you didn't."

"Then how can they convict me? They can't send an innocent man to—"

"You're an awful kid sometimes, Grey. You've got a lot to learn. Anything can happen in this old world, whether you're innocent or guilty."

"They can't do it, Judy!" he cried. "I haven't done anything. It was just a situation that . . . well, I blundered into it as usual."

"You'll come out of it," she told him with a squeeze of his hand. "It just can't be any other way—for us." The last in a voice so low he barely heard.

"For us?" he repeated heavily.

She looked up at him and smiled.

"Yes . . . for us . . Grey," she whispered. "Now I've got to go. I probably won't see you again until the trial. But I'll be thinking of you, cowboy . . . thinking and praying that you come clear . . . that some day . . ."

"Judy!" hoarsely. "I know I haven't any right . . . that we are farther apart now than ever . . . that our trails just don't seem to lead the same way. But, Judy, could I kiss you?"

For a moment she hesitated, looking at him with eyes suddenly glazed with tears. Then her lips came through the grating.

"Yes, cowboy. And it's as much for me as it is for you."

He had meant it for just a kiss to cherish in memory. But their lips clung—clung beyond thought or reason. Once he felt that firm little mouth against his, his arms went through the grating. His whole being thrilled. He was holding Judy Barrington. She was crying. He could feel the tears against his own cheeks.

"Judy," he essayed brokenly, after a time, "I . . . love . . . you."

"I've always loved you," she sobbed. "That's why it means so much. I've tried not to, Grey. But I do."

She tore herself from his arms, stood just out of reach. With fingers that trembled she dabbed at her cheeks, wiped her eyes. Then she drew herself up proudly, a trim, little figure that challenged his thoughts.

"It's all been a dream, cowboy," she said. "But now, at last, we've got something to dream about. God forgive us if it's wrong, for I just can't help it."

She whirled and was gone, leaving him gripping the bars with fingers that were white and bloodless.

Chapter XVII

Grim grey walls encompassed him, walls stained where rain had whipped through rattling window-frames and trickled down over warped aprons. Rows of scarred seats that seemed to back endlessly into a great abyss lay within the range of his vision. Above him was the judge—a pouchy-cheeked oldster with thin white hair and florid, pitted face. Unfortunately Grey sized up people at a glance, formed instant likes or dislikes. Because of these spontaneous opinions he realized that sometimes he antagonized others mentally. But for all of him he could not help disliking that judge.

The prosecutor was not such a bad sort—tall, gawky, a typical law student spilled from a mediocre school to come to carve his fortune in a small town and remain to dry rot. But before the trial ended Grey swore an oath that some day he would make that official retract every misstatement and apologize for his vitriolic abuse.

The defence lawyer, Jay Mortimer, sauntered about the court-room. He eyed the crowd with disdain, took no pains to conceal his feeling of superiority. But his arrogant manner, his urbanity failed utterly to impress the judge, who from the outset remanded him to order and overruled his objections.

Alice, stunningly dressed in black, sat beside Grey. Occasionally she leaned over to pat his arm reassuringly or whisper something to Mortimer, just ahead of her. But Grey scarcely heard. No longer now need he lie to himself. He had eyes only for Judy, seated directly opposite. When their gazes met, hers seemed to soften in a sweet, rapt expression. That expression could mean but one thing. She loved him, would stick by him to the end.

Through endless hours the selection of the jury dragged, the efforts of the impatient judge hampered by challenges and the bickering of Mortimer, who, it seemed to Grey, constantly deviated from his course on the advice of Alice. He tried to hold his tongue. At times, in his nervousness, it was almost beyond him.

Challenges . . . innuendos . . . threats . . . muttered oaths. By the end of the first day, spent in twirling his thumbs and twisting in his chair, the thing had revolved itself into a terrible farce.

"For God's sake, why don't they think of the man charged with the crime?" he protested to Mortimer, who, with Alice, had come back to the jail with him. "After all, he's the one who endures the agony of this ordeal—not you lawyers nor the spectators. I've sat and squirmed until I'm half crazy. What in hell kind of a show do you call this?"

"It's for your own good, Grey," Alice said reproachfully, taking his arm with fingers that lacked a caress. "Can't you see, Jay is using every effort to clear you?"

"I don't need every effort to clear me," he exploded. "I haven't done anything. I hate trickery and deceit in a court-room, or anywhere else."

She drew away from him, a hurt look in her eyes. "We are only doing what we think best for you."

"I know." He dropped an awkward arm about her shoulders. "And I do appreciate it. But it seems like I'll go crazy unless I get out of here— get out where I can get a breath of fresh air, where I can be free, stretch myself, get a whiff of sage-brush and grease-wood. God, I never knew before how much it meant!"

"You're as good as out, old fellow," Mortimer said reassuringly. "That judge is none too brilliant. The jury I have selected—I'll have every one of them crying before I get through with them. We'll have you free before you know it."

"Through trickery and playing on human emotions, but not because of my innocence," Grey cried. "Damn this thing they call justice. There can't be any justice until they rid the courts of rag-chewing, sneaking shysters like you."

He flung away from Alice, strode into his cell, threw himself on his cot. When, presently, he raised up, she and Mortimer had gone. He was alone—alone staring at the bare walls: walls grey, sinister, foreboding in the gathering dusk.

The second and third days of the trial were repetitions of the first.

Then, finally, after hours of heartbreaking quibble, the jury was drawn—all men, for which Grey was grateful. At least, now it was a man's game he was playing for his life, not a game where women would have any place or any hand.

On the fourth morning began the taking of testimony. Grey was thankful for this much—thankful for the August sun that streamed through the windows, forcing the bailiff to draw the torn and faded blinds to keep out the glare. Even then the curtains swung and scraped in the breeze. Grey threw back his head, took a deep breath. The vagrant breeze carried a tang of sage—sage now turning grey out on the flats of cow-land.

For the moment he forgot he was on trial for his life, forgot the drab surroundings. He was back on the Cheyenne River homestead again, loping across sun-blistered flats, the only sound the chirp of crickets, grasshoppers crackling up from under hoof. Far down in the mud-holes he seemed to catch the croak of bullfrogs. And a meadow-lark was singing as it teetered on the tip of a sage-brush, its breast flaming yellow in the sun.

Meadow-larks! How he had loved to hear them as a boy! They heralded the end of long, dreary winters, meant new life for man and beast, gave them something to look forward to after endless weeks of death-dealing blizzards and snow.

Now the thin, shrill note of the meadow-lark's happy song was drifting into the court-room. Grey's eyes flew to Judy. She, too, had heard it, was leaning forward, listening. She smiled at him reassuringly. That look, the song of the meadow-lark, gave him hope—the first hope he had felt since that last night back at the Cross Anchor.

One witness after another made their nervous way to the stand, took the oath, faltered through contradictory answers to the questions of the sharp-shooting lawyers. The State's attorney worked them easily, drawing from them admissions that, at the best, were only the wildest sort of conjecture. But Mortimer, with coat peeled and sleeves rolled up, tied them up hopelessly, left them bewildered and floundering, then openly branded them perjurers as they slunk from the stand.

Grey found himself boiling inwardly. The witnesses were not there to convict him. The testimony of many would have helped him, he thought. But his own lawyer was deliberately making a laughing-stock of them by his quick wit and shrewd brain, tearing their stories to shreds, forcing them to admit they scarcely knew what they were talking about. The whole procedure seemed unfair, a part of the farce being staged about him, his life—for which he alone seemed to care—in the balance.

The meadow-lark again! Its saucy little song rose above the sounds in the court-room—a happy, carefree note of melody.

The State had concluded. Mortimer was calling defence witnesses. Grey heard his character plated with silver, heard the story of his life— in which there was no blemish—set forth as an ideal for the passing parade. The ordinary things he had done around the ranch were pictured as deeds of heroism—even to the riding of Widow-Maker. The very life he led was exemplary, fraught with danger from the moment he rose until, dead-tired, he dragged himself to his bed. The thing sickened him. He found himself pitying the witnesses more than he pitied himself—all but the Van Ressalder and Truebolt women. He had enjoyed their discomfiture, laughed aloud when the voluble Mrs. Van Ressalder—so adept at spreading poison-gossip—became hopelessly twisted half-way through her testimony and begged to be excused. But she had not been spared. Like all the rest, she was brow-beaten, abused, cajoled—tricked into perjury by smooth-talking lawyers who had nothing at stake but a fee, Grey thought. And, in the case of Mortimer, he had no doubt that fee would be ample.

A sudden notion brought him leaning across Alice's arm.

"What's he charging me?" he asked in a lowered voice.

"Us," she corrected, smilingly. "Fifty thousand."

"Fifty thousand!" His tone was hollow. For the moment he was fearful it had carried to every part of the court-room. "My God, Alice, it will take me the rest of my life to pay that much—if I ever can."

"And about three minutes for me to write the cheque and get the cash," she said. "Don't worry. It will be taken care of."

She had turned away from him, as though the whole thing had been decided definitely. But it was far from settled in his mind. It suddenly became his chief worry, far greater even than the outcome of the trial. Fifty thousand dollars! The earnings of a lifetime for most men flipped away for the defence of Grey Sage—flipped away by his wife, the wife to whom he would always be indebted.

Barrington took the stand—a huge, graceful man, garbed in chaps and high-heeled boots polished until they glistened. A fine-looking fellow, was the thought that came to Grey. The big cowboy eyed his inquisitors coolly, took his own time to answering their questions. Of all the rest he alone appeared to be utterly at ease. Grey envied him that composure. There was something about big Hugh to envy. His confidence, which at times reached the point of arrogance, was an asset to which few men could lay claim.

Hugh defended him at every turn, Grey thought —defended him in a convincing sort of way, now shouting at the State's attorney, now shaking his fist under Mortimer's nose to send the defence lawyer leaping back. Nobody got very far with the former foreman of the Cross Anchor. If Hugh Barrington had fear of either lawyer—or anything else, for that matter—he did not show it. Nor did he change his story. He told what he knew apparently and stuck to it. His answers to the rapid-fire questions were supplied with an amazing ease, as though Hugh had memorized those answers and was reciting them.

Neither attorney cared long to question Barrington. It was obvious that both had met their master in the big cowboy. Several times titters running round the court-room brought an admonition from the judge.

Grey smiled grimly to himself. Good old Hugh! He had proved his friendship.

"That cowboy wrecked our case," he caught Mortimer's whisper to Alice. "Unless we can counteract his testimony—"

"What does he mean?" Grey cut in to demand in an undertone.

"Hugh has hurt us," Alice told him. "Didn't you hear him say that you and uncle had hated each other from the day you met, that threats had passed between you? If that testimony cannot be disproved, the case resolves itself into one of premeditated murder."

"But he told the truth," Grey whispered angrily. "That's what he swore he'd do. Damn it all, do we all have to lie to get justice? I didn't kill your uncle."

"That's what we are trying to prove." The girl's voice was weary. "But another witness like Hugh and . . ." She turned back to answer a question by Mortimer. Damn him, Grey thought; he leaned entirely too close to her. His arm was resting on hers. A glance passed between them. Grey's nerves tensed.

Instinctively his eyes sought those of Judy. There he saw a new fear. And, he noticed, she got up and left Barrington when he came swaggering back from the witness-stand. Came to Grey a flash of wonder if Barrington suspected his love for Judy—if he had heard or seen something. Yet he recalled almost word for word the big cowboy's testimony. It was the truth. There had been bad blood between Harmon and himself from the start. Where, then, had Barrington hurt him? But Mortimer's manner was visibly nervous and upset.

Interminable hours, days that seemed weeks to Grey Sage, and the witnesses had been heard. The doctor, the coroner had repeated the same monotonous rigmarole of the inquest. Others had come and gone, climbing down from the witness-chair with a sigh of relief that the mental torture of trying to remember before the staring eyes of those in the court-room had finally ended. The State summed up. Grey's ears burned at the abuse. He cringed mentally at the insinuations hurled at him. He heard himself branded a murderer, a liar, a thankless ingrate. Several times he started to his feet, fists clenched, only to be dragged back down by Alice.

Then Mortimer had the floor. In a voice that carried a sob he had drawn Grey's history—sometimes with a veiled sarcasm that made Grey boil. He pictured the simple country lad who had ridden out from nowhere to make good . . . uneducated . . . a comparative babe as far as the ways of the world outside his Wyoming range were known. It was nauseating to Grey, that sob-drawing fabrication. It seemed that Mortimer was deliberately trying to brand him in the eyes of Alice, who, he noticed, kept her face averted.

Then came the time in Mortimer's story when Grey had won honours at the Arapahoe Stampede. As though timed as a contradiction to Mortimer's words, the sheriff handed him a letter. He opened it fearfully. It was from Brown, the rodeo secretary. Harmon's protest had stood with the National Association. The charts had shown he had not won the world's championship aboard

Widow-Maker. He groaned inwardly. But what the hell difference did it make now? Damn Harmon! Damn them all!

Through the disappointment of the moment he heard Mortimer. After the Arapahoe ride, the lawyer was saying, Grey Sage, the victim of circumstances, had gone on to the Cross Anchor, flushed with his first victory. He had fallen in love with the heiress. Stunned though he was by Brown's letter, the word-picture made Grey furious. He was not a world champion—for all his effort. And he had set his heart on it. He'd show them . . . show Mortimer, the coyote. Thus far he had endured his barbs in silence. But he resolved to call the lawyer to account.

He closed his ears to the infernal taunting of the plea. He noticed a juror swiping at his eyes. Another was fumbling for his kerchief. Still another was polishing his glasses. Mortimer's voice rose and fell, now vibrant, trembling, now low, tearful. Alice was crying. Judy was crying. Stifled sobs came from the courtroom as the picture of him, Grey Sage, the poor country boy, was dragged before the vision of the morbidly curious onlookers. The State's attorney had taken to striding about, as though to distract the attention of the jurors. Mortimer only waxed more and more eloquent. But what the hell difference did it make? He, Grey Sage, had been beaten out of a world championship, when he could ride any horse they had. He had proved it at the Cross Anchor aboard Widow-Maker. He'd show them . . . the damned cheap skates who protested rides!

A sudden lull brought Grey back to a sense of things about him. Mortimer had taken his seat. The State's attorney had plunged into the rebuttal—like a dog leaping at a fallen rabbit, Grey thought. But harangue and fume, spout and threaten as he did, his plea fell on deaf ears. The jury was still under the spell of Mortimer's sob story. Grey buried his face in his hands in shame that he had countenanced such a defence for a crime he had not committed. But it was too late now. The jury, the crowd pitied him, were crying for him. He fought down a wild impulse to leap up, tell them all to go to hell. Instead, he kept his face covered. Nor did he raise his eyes until the jury had received its instructions and filed out.

The judge was preparing to leave. Grey was vaguely aware that he was giving orders where to call him. The sheriff was stepping forward to return Grey to his cell. He rose mechanically, fighting against a blazing desire to smash his fist into the leering face of Mortimer. Then he was in the jam beside the sheriff. No word had passed between him and Alice. He had left her abruptly at the table—with Mortimer, he remembered.

Of a sudden the crowd halted. The judge was

returning to the bench, was rapping loudly for order. The sheriff turned. Grey was not interested. He had seen and heard all he wanted to of the farce of justice. If he were to hang, what difference did it make now? He had lost the championship because of a spiteful protest. Here in the court-room he had been shamed until he could never look any one in the face again. He had made a mess of things. All the things he had longed for were gone. He had no one to thank but himself. The trial . . conviction . . . death seemed a fitting penalty.

"The jury is back already," the sheriff was saying excitedly, dragging at his arm. "It may be a verdict. If it is, it is the quickest in the history of—"

Grey heard his name called. It was the judge. With a poor attempt to collect himself, measure his steps, he walked towards the bench. The foreman of the jury, which had filed into the box, was dabbing at his eyes.

"We, the jury, find Grey Sage not guilty." The verdict came haltingly.

Pandemonium broke loose. The judge rapped vainly for order. The sheriff was slapping Grey on the back. The crowd, particularly the guests from the Cross Anchor, were closing in on him, all talking at once. Mrs. Van Ressalder and Mrs. Truebolt, the old scandalmongers, even the judge was offering his hand. The thing bewildered

Grey. Exonerated! But his pleasure was lessened by the knowledge that it had not been the evidence, not the straightforward testimony in his favour, not his own clear conscience. For his freedom he had to thank the heart-rending plea of Jay Mortimer.

"I'm glad, cowboy," came Judy's whispered voice—"so darned glad I can't hold back the tears much longer. Glad for you—and glad for us. So-long, cowboy." He whirled to stop her. In his joy he wanted only her to share it. He needed her. But Judy had been swallowed up in the crowd.

He broke away, started for the ante-room. He had seen Alice and Mortimer go in that direction.

From office to office he went. He could not locate them. Presently he heard her voice, low, guarded, he thought, beyond a partly opened door just off the judge's chambers.

"Mort," she was saying in a tone that struck a chill to Grey's heart, "you were wonderful . . . marvellous."

Grey Sage stepped inside. His wife . . . Alice . . . was in Mortimer's arms. Their lips were pressed tightly together.

They leaped away from one another, whirled to regard him guiltily. He stood stock still, sweeping them with blazing eyes. When he spoke he attempted to keep the anger from his voice.

"You were all right," he got out raspingly. "Thanks."

Mortimer made the mistake of taking his remark for cowardice.

"Keep your thanks," he sneered. "You're as guilty as hell. I only saved your worthless hide for Alice's sake."

Grey Sage recoiled. The thing numbed him: numbed him beyond sense or reason. With a primitive instinct, his fists doubled. He caught hold of himself. One fight had ended disastrously. To start another now, in the shadow of the judge's bench . . . he dared not . . . not even for Alice. After all, was she worth it?

He spun on his heel, strode outside, banged the door shut behind him. A few paces and he stopped. For the life of him he couldn't swallow the accusation, couldn't countenance the thing he had seen. He whirled, started back. Cool reason tempered hasty judgment. With a mighty effort he heaved himself away from the door, stalked down the corridor. Behind lay heartaches, more trouble; ahead lay freedom.

Outside he threw back his chest, inhaled deeply of the soft, balmy night air. The meadow-larks could sing now . . . if only he could find Judy.

Chapter XVIII

Never afterwards was Grey Sage able to recall his trip to the Cross Anchor. Although he was vaguely aware that he had somehow secured a horse, he moved like a man in a dream, prey to conflicting emotions that ran riot within him. Only the swift pace of his mount and the night wind whipping his face seemed to ease the tumult in his soul. Now he was seeing red, murder in his heart, now cursing himself for a blundering idiot. He had lost the championship; he was stabbed with remorse at losing Alice, in the same breath murmuring the name of Judy. Out of the chaos of his thoughts came one question that beat on his brain. Could a man love two women?

He had no answer for it. In spite of his fear of her, he did love Alice in a timid way. He knew now what had prompted that fear. It was her money, her education, her position. He laughed aloud—a harsh sound that set his horse to shying off the trail. But there was still the matter of the fifty thousand to pay Mortimer. He'd pay it. But . . . damn Mortimer. The fellow had held Alice, his wife, in his arms . . . had kissed her.

Then, like a thunderbolt, came the meaning of Alice's remark the night of their marriage in Arapahoe. She had said that she had not quite been married. She hadn't. But she had loved Mortimer. There probably had been an engagement, and Alice had married him, Grey Sage, to spite Mortimer.

Damn her! Damn him! Mortimer could have her. He had them to thank for nothing—only a trial for a crime he did not commit. Alice herself could be guilty. Until now he had never let himself entertain such an unworthy thought. But he had left her in the room with Harmon. And he had lied to save her at the trial. In his furious anger, he did not doubt that she would stoop to murder. What had become of Judy? How he wanted her—if only to feel her fingers in his! The mere contact of her hand bolstered up the courage he needed so badly at the moment.

He would locate Barrington, who had once asked him to become a partner in the wild string. He still had most of the money he had won. And there was Harmon's cheque for losing the bet on Widow-Maker. He'd collect that. And his salary . . . he had spent none of it. That much would start him. He would join Barrington—and Judy. Yet could he travel with them and still remember she was the wife of his friend?

His horse pushed the miles behind it with amazing ease. He was at the gate of the Cross Anchor. The big place was ablaze with lights. Most of the guests had returned by car from the trial. He could tell by the shouts and music they

183

were having a hilarious time. After the sob story Mortimer had given to the jury, he hated to face them. But he must gather together his few things and tell Alice he was leaving. He would sign a note with Mortimer for defending him. After that . . . no, he'd be damned if he would sign a note.

He was down at the barn, had led his horse inside, fed it. Then he was going towards the house, determined to see the thing through. On the veranda he hesitated. It took almost more nerve than he possessed to bring himself to face that crowd.

He strode across the veranda, threw open the door. At his sudden entrance the hilarity ceased. The crowd inside came surging forward, shouting his name, crying out words of commendation.

This sudden interest abashed him. He halted, scarcely knowing what to do.

"We're glad, Sage," one man said with sincerity. "Glad, because we knew you didn't do it."

"Where's your bride?" another shouted. "I'll bet she's happy."

"She'll be along after a time, I reckon," Grey said with a sinking sensation. "Go ahead and have a good time, folks. But I reckon I'm the one who is really happy at being cleared."

He started away. The men seized hold of him.

"No you don't," one muttered thickly. "They talk about the hospitality of the range, and we've never even had a drink with you. Here's where you make yourself sociable. If you'd take charge of this ranch you couldn't hire enough wranglers to handle the crowd."

Never before had Grey been told anything like this. And it gave him a feeling of satisfaction. After all, these men—and perhaps the women, too—had noticed him. Yet they had never seemed over-friendly. Perhaps it had been himself.

"All of us have wanted to knock around with you. You never gave us a chance. We'd about decided you had your head swelled because you were a great bronc-rider." Liquor had loosened the fellow's tongue. "A man can't live within himself like you're trying to do. He has to have buddies to unload on, or he'll go crazy. Hell, man, there's nothing wrong with you. You just won't let yourself make friends. We're real, even though we don't wear spurs and bowleg when we walk. We like you cowboys, although we don't think you're a damned bit better than we are. We don't turn dude, as you call us, on account of you. We turn dude for your Western atmosphere, to enjoy your country, not your men or women. As far as cowboys go, we've got some of the finest in the world right along the Hudson River. Want to come back and see?"

"No, thanks."

Grey laughed—the first laugh he had had in what seemed years. It made him feel better. He was among friends. Any one who would talk to him thus could be nothing but a friend. There was no doubting this group, even though they had been drinking. And to think he always had been half fearful of them. Never before had he found this free-and-easy comradeship with any one—not even old Mason. He realized suddenly that lack of friends was the cause of his loneliness. In his retiring, self-conscious way—he could see it now—he had never proffered friendship, had never given any one an opportunity to get close to him. He had often envied the fellows towards whom—without apparent effort on their part—people seemed to gravitate. And now they were doing the same with him. Yet there was a difference. Before, he had been but a dude wrangler, an ordinary cowboy who attracted no more than passing interest. Now he was a man who had been dragged through a murder trial.

They were at the bar. His new-found friends were ordering strange drinks. The bar-tender was caroming glasses in every direction. Although never a drinker like men of the West, he had no objection to it, he now found keen enjoyment in the new and easy companionship about him. A half-dozen of the warming drinks and he was talking freely with them all—talking freely for the first time in his life. Several of the women in the group had joined the crowd. Someone started a song. Grey joined in, although for a moment his temerity startled him.

Glasses upraised, they were trying to harmonize. One of the girls moved closer to him. His arm fell about her shoulders. He scarcely noticed that she cuddled under the caress, edged nearer.

They were singing loudly now, without much tune, but to their own discordant ears capable of perfect harmony. Unused to liquor and slightly unsteady in the knees, Grey pulled away and sat down. The others crowded round, keeping him always the centre of attraction. The girls, too, had flocked about him. One had settled herself on his knee. Another had an arm round his neck. They were singing the old songs with a keen sense of enjoyment.

Into this group walked Alice and Mortimer. Alice swept the crowd with a startled look. A sneer twisted Mortimer's lips. The things he had seen that afternoon suddenly surged back into Grey's mind. He pushed the girls roughly aside, got to his feet. He tried to get his half-emptied glass on the bar. The bar wasn't there. The glass shattered on the floor. The resounding crash grated on nerves suddenly grown taut. Grey looked about.

Then he was laughing. But he was scarcely aware of it. Yet his anger had vanished. What did he care for Mortimer?

He started to lurch out from the crowd. Some-one jerked him back.

"Don't make another fool of yourself, cowboy; you've done enough damage for to-day."

It was Judy. From where she had come he did not know. But sight of her sobered him. He turned to look in her eyes. They were bitterly accusing.

"I'm sorry," he said thickly. "Let's go outside a minute."

She piloted him to the door, past Mortimer, who stepped aside. Alice had gone on, for which he was thankful. The crowd was shouting after him.

"Can't stand any more." He waved back to them. "Need air. See you later."

A laugh went up. Then he was outside leaning on the rail of the veranda, with Judy beside him. She was staring away into the far dark—into the heavens splashed with a myriad of stars.

"You can't do those things, Grey," she was chiding in a low tone. "Drink makes a fool of some men. You're one of them. Besides, you don't belong in that crowd."

"What crowd do I belong in?" he cried. "I was only trying to meet these people . . . trying to find some one I really could call friend. If I'd known you were here—"

"I know." She moved closer to him. "You haven't done anything wrong. But I saw that look you gave Mortimer. I was afraid."

"You needn't be. But, damn Mortimer. If I join Hugh in the wild-horse string do you suppose you and I could . . . stay apart?"

"It would be mighty hard, but we could try

though. I'd love to have you in with Hugh, love to be travelling with you. But . . . Hugh is awfully jealous."

"He's got a right to be. He has a mighty pretty wife."

"To some people, perhaps. But I don't need watching. I never look at another man, except—"

"And I don't want you to. Shall we try it, Judy?"

"If we saw it wouldn't work, we might make excuses," she murmured. "I could leave, or you—"

"It's a go, then," he said happily. "This is my last night here. Where can I locate Hugh?"

"He went to Belle Fourche, up in the Black Hills. He'll be there for a couple of weeks. We can catch him there."

"We?"

"I'm to meet him there. I thought perhaps we might go together."

He captured her gaze.

"If we go through with this thing, we are going to play fair," he said. "You know as well as I do, we wouldn't dare travel . . ."

"I know," she said contritely, her eyes falling. "It was a wish, not sane judgment, that prompted me to say that. You go on . . . catch Hugh at Belle Fourche. I'll come along later. I'm going to ride, you know . . . going to go back into the rodeo contests."

"I don't know whether you are or not."

"I've talked Hugh into it. After all, he's my . . . forgive me," quickly, seizing his hand. "I didn't mean it that way. Don't be so sensitive, Grey. You're always getting your feelings hurt. If you're going to act like this, I'll never agree to letting you come into the wild-horse string."

"There is nothing you can say or do to stop me," he said with assurance. "There is nothing you would say or do to stop me—from anything. Is there?"

"No." Now her fingers were toying with the lapel of his coat. Her body was pressed close. "No, Grey, unless it is something like back there at the bar."

Her arms slipped up round his neck. She was standing on tiptoe, looking into his eyes.

"I don't know why this thing should have come to me. But I love you, Grey. I'd do almost anything for you."

"And I love you, Judy." He stroked her hair lovingly. "I hope . . ."

What he was about to say was never finished. Their lips met in a long and delicious kiss that left them both trembling.

She drew away presently.

"I'm going to my room now," she whispered. "This will be good-bye until I join you and Hugh."

"Good-bye."

Then he was alone, looking out into the prairie darkness. It was there a boy found him.

"Your wife wishes to speak with you, sir . . . in the office."

Grey snapped out his cigarette, went inside. The noisy group at the bar had thinned down. Waving to them, he passed on to the office. There he found Alice and Mortimer.

He halted just inside, looking at them.

"Come in, please, Grey," Alice invited. "And close the door."

Without answering he obeyed, moved up until he stood directly above them.

Chapter XIX

"Why don't you say something?" Alice asked nervously.

"There isn't anything to say, is there?" Grey finally pinned the roving gaze of Mortimer.

"The matter of a settlement . . ." Mortimer found his voice. ". . . and the divorce."

"Settlement . . . divorce? What are you talking about?"

"Why, Alice's property . . . I presume you married her for money?"

"Jay!" Alice cried in affright.

The lawyer had risen to his feet, stood as tall and well-knit as Grey himself. And, Grey sensed, the muscles beneath his modish clothes had not grown flabby from disuse. Those muscles had fought an oar, had been strengthened by football. By no means did Grey under-estimate this man before him, although he did boil with sudden anger at his question.

"I didn't marry Alice for money," he blurted out. "I didn't marry Alice."

"Didn't marry her?" Mortimer's tone was biting. "Of course, if you were trying to pull something . . ."

Grey's fury burst all bounds. He leaped forward. Alice pushed in between them.

"Don't be a fool, Jay," she reprimanded. "You're not talking to a cheap cowhand."

"Who has the goods on you proper if he wants to push it," Grey shot in, although he was instantly sorry for the remark. "Now if you want to talk sense, walloper, shoot. If not, get out!"

"Get out!" Mortimer exploded. "What do you mean?"

"Just what I said."

Now Grey had complete control of himself, was almost enjoying the thing. He liked to see Mortimer squirm: Mortimer who obviously was covering his nervousness with bluff, as he had done in the court-room. He had put it across then because the witnesses had been terrified half out of their senses by the surroundings and his heartless questioning. Here it was different. Mortimer was the under-dog. And, Grey knew, the lawyer was smart enough to realize it.

"I happen to be married to Alice Harmon—in spite of the fact that I found her kissing you in that office." Grey exulted at sight of the girl cringing away from him. "And I happen to be head of this ranch right at the minute. Now I'm telling you, you either talk turkey or get off the Cross Anchor."

"There's no need for further threats," Alice put in. "This thing can all be settled amicably. After all, it isn't as though we . . ." She bit her lip, abruptly halted what she was about to say.

"Jay was just trying to find out what you wanted."

"I still don't know what you are driving at."

"I want to know, my dear fellow," Mortimer said in a tone of deep exasperation, "just why you married Alice? You didn't love her. You are in love with—Judy Barrington!"

Grey couldn't hold in any longer. His fist shot out, landed flush on Mortimer's jaw. The lawyer went down like a log. Alice uttered a little shriek, dropped to her knees beside him.

"You brute!" she cried. "Are you trying to commit another murder?"

Stark, cruel rage possessed Grey Sage. He leaped over beside the girl, jerked her to her feet, pushed her roughly into a chair.

"So you think I killed your uncle, even though I left this room before you did. Afterwards I was with you every minute until we came back from being married. Your uncle wasn't dead when I left. I'm not so sure about it when you . . ." For all his anger he got no satisfaction from her violent start, her fear-widened eyes, her stifled sobs. But they did not silence him. "I know you two . . . I can see it all now . . . see what you meant when you said you'd never been quite married. It's him you're in love with. You married me to spite him . . . and the same night needed him to get you out of a jam. You haven't been pulling the wool over my eyes." He stood above the girl, who stared at him with terror-widened eyes.

"I didn't marry you," he blazed. "You married me . . . and I'm not so sure that you aren't mixed up in framing me for your uncle's death just so you could go free."

"Grey!" she cried piteously. "Please . . . not that . . . honest."

"You don't know what the word means." He sprang over to Mortimer, who was rubbing his jaw, trying to rise. "Get up and join the pow-wow," he lashed out.

The lawyer got to his feet, sidled over to a chair beside Alice.

"You asked about a settlement," Grey shot in. "Let's get down to cases. How about paying this walloper?"

"He's already paid," Alice said chokingly.

"How?" Grey demanded brutally. She flinched under it.

"I don't think . . ." Mortimer began.

"You keep your bill out." Grey stopped him. "If you could think outside of a court-room, you wouldn't be kissing other men's wives. I'm still asking how that fifty thousand was paid."

"I wrote a cheque," Alice said in a low voice that trembled. "It was part of the agreement."

"So you two had an agreement?"

"I don't know what you mean."

"Never mind. Get your cheque back."

"I won't return it," Mortimer flared. He started up furiously. "Damn you—"

"Sit down." Grey seized him by the lapels, slammed him back into the chair. "You're not in New York, jasper. You're out on the range, where men get killed for playing around with other men's wives. I said I wanted that cheque." With fingers that shook Mortimer found his wallet, extracted the cheque, passed it over. Grey tore it to bits, tossed them into the fire-place.

"Where's that cheque your uncle wrote me?" he demanded of Alice.

She pointed to the desk. Grey found it presently, in a litter of papers. He endorsed it, passed it over to Mortimer. "There is a thousand dollars . . . more than what your damned lying defence was worth to clear an innocent man. After all, you defended me, not her. I didn't hire you. I came near kicking you out of the court-room a dozen times. Now you're paid."

"I'll sue . . ." Mortimer began furiously.

"Go ahead," Grey challenged. "Make it for a million, and that will be just half what I'll ask in a counter-suit. There's a charge of alienation of affections, isn't there? I'm not very smart about law. But from what I saw of you brow-beating honest folks in that court-room, I'm not so sure I have to be smart. You're just a shyster. Now you've been paid. I want a receipt in full."

"I won't give you one."

"That's up to you, jasper. I'll just file suit tomorrow for stealing my wife's love."

"It's blackmail . . ." Mortimer cried. ". . . damnable blackmail."

"Never heard of that out here." Grey smiled—a grim smile that barely moved thin lips across his teeth. For Mortimer had crossed to the desk, whipped out a fountain-pen and was writing a receipt.

"For services in full," Grey dictated.

When the paper was written he looked at it closely. Apparently satisfied, he placed it in his pocket.

"Now you make yourself scarce around here," he hurled at Mortimer.

"He'll do nothing of the kind," Alice found her voice. "You've gone too far already. True, I did marry you to spite Jay. But I've regretted it— regretted it the minute I did it. I didn't know you then."

The utter lack of sincerity in her tone brought Grey's eyes upon her.

"Not until this shyster painted me to the jury to-day as a ragged country boy trying to make good by marrying an heiress," he raged. "But go on. Have your say. Get it off your chest. Any way you feel about me goes double."

Alice shrank back.

"We still want to know what property settlement Alice must make to quiet this thing down," Mortimer put in.

"Why should Alice make a property settlement?"

"The divorce . . . you have a husband's claim. I thought even you would know that."

"What divorce?"

"The divorce you naturally will want after what you saw this afternoon—"

Again Grey bounded forward. Mortimer leaped back.

"Don't make any cracks like that, or I'll beat you to death," Grey snarled. "I didn't see anything that would make me think any different of Alice. You're the one I blame. Just because a woman kisses a man when she is excited and thankful, doesn't mean she isn't a good woman, by a hell of a ways. Don't try to blacken this girl before me, like you blackened those witnesses. No matter what you say, I wouldn't believe . . ." He caught Alice's eyes. Tears made them misty. "I don't want any property settlement."

"Thank you, Grey," she said in a low tone. "That's the finest thing I've ever heard any man say."

"I mean it." Grey whirled on her. "You're cold . . . I'm afraid of you . . . there's something untouchable about you to me. But no man is going to say a word against you. There's no grounds for divorce as far as I'm concerned. If there were, you'd have to be the one to tell me —not someone like him."

"You can have your divorce," she said in a tone that chilled him. "And what property settlement you demand."

"Alice? Do you mean—"

"I'm not your kind." Her words came falteringly. "Let me go, Grey. You don't understand my world. I don't understand yours. I'll pay what you want. Money means nothing to me . . . I . . ." He stared in disbelief. Alice Harmon was actually crying.

Grey spun back to Mortimer.

"The divorce is up to Alice," he spat out. "If she wants it, she can get it. As for me, I have no grounds. That's our code out here in the sagebrush, jasper. Our women are white and good and clean, no matter what wallopers like you think. As for a settlement . . . to hell with her money. I don't want a cent. You squander it for her. But I do want to buy Widow-Maker."

He strode over to the door.

"I advise you to move into town until I get out of the country," he threw back at the openmouthed Mortimer. "You move or I'll—"

"Grey!" It was Alice. "Take Widow-Maker. And won't you please take something else? I want you to be independent. You can't go back as you were. Let me draw you a cheque . . . for enough to keep you the rest of your life. I've got so much, Grey."

"To hell with your money. Keep it . . . or give it to this bounder!" With that he was gone.

Chapter XX

Grey Sage rode north the following morning, the outlaw Widow-Maker tailed to a packhorse on which were strapped his bedroll and camp equipage. He left the Cross Anchor at sun-up, moved away without a word to any one save the cook who prepared him breakfast and expressed genuine regret at his departure. Outside the home pasture he drew rein to look back at the rambling ranch-house. One of those gleaming windows was in Alice's room. But there was no sign of her.

He had hoped that he might encounter Judy at the barn. For the first time, she was absent.

Somehow it seemed fitting that he should ride away as he had come—without friends, an unknown, heading back to the sage-brush. Once out from the ranch, he attempted to drive from his mind the things that lay behind. Ahead was a new world—a world that held for him success or failure.

Up across the rolling hills he jogged. Ducks wheeled overhead, frightened up from the puddles glinting on the flats. Here and there a bunch of sage-chickens, startled by his approach, soared into the air with a zooming sound that set his horses to shying. A cottontail darted down the trail ahead of him, zig-zagging as it ran. A great white jack-rabbit bounded over the brush, presently to sit on its haunches and watch him.

Far to the north swayed the Black Hills, a purple etching on a yellow skyline. To the east and west rolling plains, the sandhills of western Nebraska, cut by the verdant valley of the sluggish Platte River.

On he rode, sunk in thought that took little reckoning of time or distance, through the morning, noonday, afternoon, pausing only long enough to feed his horses from nosebags and water them at a prairie-hole. Then he went on, pushing the miles behind him.

That night he jerked off his bed-roll on the flats. Behind now lay the Casper Mountains, dim-etched on the horizon. Hobbling his horses, he turned them loose to graze and prepared his simple supper. Having eaten, he stamped out his fire and rolled into his blankets to lie gazing up at the stars that spangled the sky. Far below a coyote was howling—an eerie wail coming out of the dark: the age-old mating cry. A bull was bawling its raucous challenge to the world at large. A steer was attempting to answer that throaty rumble. For all the otherwise peaceful quiet, the night was filled with thin small sounds —the whisper of critters and insects. Overhead a Phoebe bird lent its song to the zooming of bullbats chasing bugs in the lowering light.

In spite of his weariness, sleep eluded him. He lay mulling over the events that had crowded down upon him, random thoughts that persisted until his brain was in a whirl. The trial—who really had killed Harmon? He had resolved to remain on the ranch until he had found the real killer. He had ridden away without so much as giving the mystery a thought. Alice . . . Mortimer . . . vivid recollection of the last trying scene set him to tossing in his blankets, fired within him hot anger. Far different from those dreams of Judy . . . for he could close his eyes and see her with a glad sort of feeling.

She danced across his mental vision like a creature of some fairy glade, always smiling at him, beckoning him on. He wondered if the time would ever come when he dared hope to have Judy for his wife. He wanted her so. Yet so many things stood between them.

The new sun, tipping the buttes to drench the prairie with a fling of vivid colour, found him already on the trail—north towards the low-flung etching that was the Black Hills. And on the way he would stop at his homestead. He would see Mason, yet he dreaded that meeting now that he had made such a mess of things. Somehow he knew that Mason would understand.

On the evening of the fifth day he let down the gate to old Mason's pasture, replaced it, led his horses to the shack. The cowman hobbled to the door, peered at him through faded eyes. With a shout, he came forth.

"Grey . . . Grey Sage!" He was hanging to the youth's hand. "Am I glad to see you! Been thinking about you, kid. Stable your horses. Are you back to stay? Toss your roll right here in the house." He paused for lack of breath.

Grey smiled. Old Mason was sincerely glad to see him—the only person in the world who would be glad, except perhaps, Judy . . . maybe Brown . . . and Mrs. Brown . . . Barrington. After all, there were lots of people who would be glad to see him now that he thought of it. He really was not so much alone as he had made himself believe.

He stabled and cared for his horses and went into the shack. Mason had started supper. A glorious repast for the old cowman, bacon strips sizzling on the stove, fried potatoes. Mason had even celebrated so far as to stir up a small cake. Real cooks, these old cowhands, Grey thought—men who cooked little, but who could, on occasion, prepare a meal fit for a king. Here was friendship—the friendship he craved. It assuaged the hurt that lay within him at recollection of Alice and Mortimer.

"So you're the champion bronc-rider," old Mason was chattering. "The paper at the county seat made a big to-do about it . . . printed your picture . . . told all about your paw and maw.

That's great, kid. I knew you had it in you. And you did it so quick."

"I didn't win top honours," Grey said bitterly. "My ride was protested."

"That's too bad," Old Mason peered at the youth's lean face, at the eyes staring out across the prairie seeing nothing. "You've been hurt, kid. A woman?"

"Don't amount to anything," carelessly. But Grey's carelessness did not for a minute deceive his friend.

"Tell me, kid . . . get it off your chest before it eats your heart out."

"Yes, it's a woman."

"Married?"

"Yes."

"Tell old Mason!"

"There isn't much to tell."

Grey slumped down on one of the benches he had known so well when he was a boy. His idle gaze swept the dingy cabin. There was the same cracked mirror, the same sheet-iron stove casting off its smell of rancid grease, the same pictures of women, the same cans stuck about on the rough studding. He couldn't live in these surroundings again. He hated such an existence, pitied those who were forced to put up with it. His life lay in far places! Places where he could see something, do things differently. Yet, for all its uninviting interior, there was something homey about it—something that tugged at his heartstrings.

"I'm . . . married, Mason," he said.

"Married?" The grizzled cowhand flipped the bacon with pancake turner! "Who is she? Where is she?"

"Back at the Cross Anchor—a dude ranch in the Casper mountains."

"Then she's a Western girl. Good for you, kid! I knew you'd do it." He hobbled over to slap Grey on the back.

"She isn't a Western girl. She's an Easterner. Owns the big dude ranch. Worth a million or more. But we've split up."

Once in it, he unburdened himself with a rush, as though trying to rid himself of some awful thing. Mason listened without interruption, the while he took up the bacon and potatoes and placed them on the table. From the oven he drew a pan of biscuits, the cake, poured the coffee for both of them, sat down and began eating.

Grey's outburst concluded, silence fell between them. The only sound was the crackle of hoppers in the yard, the distant lowing of cattle and the old cowhand munching his food.

"Too bad," Mason commented grimly. "But just one of those things a fellow gets in. I suppose you love her—that's why you're eating your heart out for her."

"No!"

"But there's a woman behind your eyes."

"Not her." Grey was conscious of shame at the admission. "It's another woman, Mason. I married Alice. But I love . . . Judy. I've made a mess of the whole damned thing . . . and I've taken just these few weeks to do it in."

"You wrote me about this Alice and Judy. She's—"

"Hugh Barrington's wife!"

"You sure did the job up brown." The old cowman's observation was sour. "You couldn't have got into much more hell in this short time no matter who you were; that's a cinch. And you were tried for murder?"

"You know about that, too?"

"The county seat paper had it. 'Local Boy Cleared of Murder!' The biggest type they had in the office, I reckon. Hadn't been used for so long it had whiskers. You've sure built up a reputation, haven't you?"

"Reckon I have. But I'm going to live it down. I'm going to buy in with Barrington in this wild string."

"And have a blow-up with him over his wife," Mason remarked sagely. "It'll never work, kid. The farther you stay away from this Barrington, the better off you'll be. Let's get back to that other thing. Who killed this Harmon?"

"I don't know, and I don't care."

"Strikes me that's a poor way to look at it

when you were tried for murder." There was mild rebuke in the tone. "Even though you were cleared, there are those who still think you did it—always will think so until the real killer is brought to time. Give me the lowdown. Let's see if there isn't a lead an old jasper like me can ferret out."

With minute detail Grey described the scene leading up to the finding of Harmon's body, repeated almost word for word their conversation in the office that night before he left after the fight.

"And Alice—your wife—stayed behind for a minute?" Mason asked.

"Yes, but—"

"Then she did it, sure as shooting," Mason announced positively.

"No, she didn't," Grey defended. "In the first place, if she had, she'd have had a gun or a club of some kind, and it would have been in the room. In the second place, her grief was real when she came back from town and was told about the thing. Somebody else killed Harmon, Mason. But who?"

"Puzzling, ain't it?" The cowman scratched his thatch of grey hair. "Kind of challenges a feller. I wouldn't rest until I'd figured it out."

"It's not worrying me," Grey said. "All I want is to get out of the mess I've made of things. You don't think a tie-up with Barrington will work?"

"Figure it out for yourself. You admit you love his wife. She loves you, so you think. You're both married. How long will it be before this Barrington gets wise? If he's jealous, he'll probably kill you or her or both of you."

"There'll be nothing like that."

"That's what you say now. But you're fooling yourself. Men and women aren't built that way. They're weak—awful weak."

"But I didn't kill Mortimer when I caught him kissing Alice," Grey defended lamely.

"You didn't love her enough. If you had, you'd have gone stark raving mad and probably had another murder charge to face. No, kid, it's never going to work. But I suppose you'll try it."

"It's either that or come back to the homestead. I'd go crazy back here now. I reckon it's a thing a fellow can't take advice on, no matter if he knows the advice is right. I've made up my mind to go with Hugh."

"Then all I can say is for you to keep your eye peeled, because a hell-fire ruckus is going to break loose when you least expect it."

While he was talking, Mason had been wolfing his food after the manner of men who eat alone. Grey had eaten little. A few mouthfuls that seemed to choke him, and he pushed it away to light a cigarette. The old cowman noticed. He was hurt. Grey knew it, but said nothing.

Once through, Mason cleared up the dishes, set

about washing them. Grey dried them. Presently they were outside, seated on the stoop gazing into the gathering gloom. Far down the river the flats ran together in a purple line—a sea of purple that bathed the entire region in a soft and eerie light. For the moment it stirred Grey, reminded him of . . . but those days were passed. He could still drink in the beauty of the prairies, but the infernal loneliness was an ever-present torment to his soul.

Time and again he was tempted to chuck the whole affair and remain. Yet he could not bring himself to do it. He had quaffed too deeply of the cup of adulation in the outside world. Never again would he be satisfied with this narrow life on the range. Besides, there were so many things he could do out there now. Where but a few short weeks ago he had drawn back from facing the world because of an inherent timidity, he now looked out upon it with the eyes of a conqueror— the eyes of a man who had within him the power to master and dominate, to win endless laurels, the plaudits of the multitude.

For a time they sat in silence, Grey smoking one cigarette after another.

Old Mason dragged contentedly on a wheezing pipe that sent up clouds of rank smoke.

"Why don't this Judy divorce Barrington and marry you if she loves you?"

Grey started at the frank question.

"She couldn't. I'm married too."

"But you're going to get a divorce?"

"No."

"Why?"

"I wouldn't give Mortimer that much satisfaction." The old fellow dropped a gnarled hand on his shoulder.

"There's nothing in life that will warp a man's soul like hate and revenge, kid," he said in a solemn tone. "They're two things every man who amounts to anything must rise above. In refusing a divorce to your wife, you're not only wrecking her life but your own. Can't you see you're not hurting her as much as you're hurting yourself? If you were free, perhaps this Judy and you—"

"I'll not give her a divorce until I get damned good and ready," Grey said stubbornly.

"It may be too late for your own happiness, kid."

"I never thought of it that way," Grey admitted, suddenly swayed by the argument. "But, what grounds could I get a divorce on?"

"This fellow Mortimer . . . you say you saw her kissing him? He stayed at the ranch while you were in jail?"

"Do you think I'd sue for divorce on such grounds?" the youth flamed. "I'd be willing to let things ride as they are for the rest of my life before I'd do a thing like that. There was nothing wrong. Alice may be cold but she's good. Nobody can tell me any different."

"You still love her a little, don't you?" Mason peered at him in the lowering light.

"I don't know. But I'll never divorce her on the grounds you mention. After all, she's a good woman. We cowhands do respect women."

"That we do, kid," old Mason said. "But she may have an angle. It takes a big man, a fine man to look at every side of a question. Did you ever think of letting her have the divorce?"

"How?"

"Why, desertion, of course. You've deserted her, haven't you?"

"She could get it on those grounds, at that," Grey mused. "Mebbeso I'll write her and suggest it. If it wasn't for that damned Mortimer."

"You'll run across Mortimers all your life," Mason said drily. "The world is full of them. The mark of a real man is in being able to look over the heads of the Mortimers. Just what are you aiming to do first?"

"Go on to Belle Fourche and join up with Hugh. I've got Widow-Maker here—the horse you read about me qualifying on—the worst bucker in the rodeos. And I've got a few hundred dollars with which to buy new wild stock. Hugh could handle the contract end of it. I could go round the country buying new horses."

"But you're the top rider in the game. A young

fellow in his prime. Are you going to let a protest keep you from winning the championship? t don't seem fittin' and right, kid."

"I want that title more than anything else in the world," Grey said. "I'll win it all right. Then, when I get too old to ride, I'll have the wild string."

"I wonder if you will," Mason said, getting painfully to his feet and knocking the cold ashes from his pipe against the door studding. "I'm turning in, kid. Ain't been feeling so well of late. Just unroll your bed-roll on the floor here. Goodnight."

For a long time Grey sat staring off into the darkness. Then, arising, he made sure the horses were all right, unrolled his bed out under the stars and crawled between the blankets.

Chapter XXI

Again the thrill of the rodeo was in the blood of Grey Sage—thunderous cheers, vivid colour, pounding hoofs, stifling dust.

A single night with old Mason back at the Cheyenne River shack, and he had packed his horse, tailed up Widow-Maker and come on to Belle Fourche. He had wanted to remain for a time with Mason. But somehow everything had changed. No longer could he bare his soul to his friend, as once he had done. The things the wise old fellow surmised were too near the truth. He came suddenly to the realization that he didn't want to see things as they really were. Rather he found himself vacillating between a forlorn hope that everything would work out as he had planned and a dread that it would not. After all, it was only his business if he had made a mess of things. So he had ridden away from Mason's the following dawn.

"Running away from yourself!" He seemed to hear again Alice's accusation that morning of their first ride together. Her strange words had puzzled him then. Now he knew. He was leaving old Mason not because he wanted to, but because he was afraid to face the truth.

He had cut across Robber's Roost and Alkali,

ridden up along the foothills of the Black Hills, pausing time and again to shift sidewise in his saddle and revel in the changing colours of growing day—blue and purple, red and fire yellow, a shifting panorama of light. And always now to the east were great sandstone pillars crowned with dead-white gyp rock. A glorious picture crowding up from the floor of the prairie that stretched away to the west, unbroken for countless miles.

A day . . . a night. He unrolled his tarp bed on high ground above Beaver Creek. There he slept, singularly at peace with the world. Why, he did not know. He had no reason for peace within him-self.

Next morning, to the song of meadow-larks in the sage, he cooked himself some flapjacks in the breaking dawn, saddled his horse and was gone with the sun, pushing north along the foot-hills.

The fourth day he rode into Belle Fourche. He turned over his horses to a stable groom, walked forth to mingle with the crowd—the same crowd, apparently, he had seen in Arapahoe. He seemed to recognize some of the faces. But now it was different. No longer was he the shy, almost miserable youth who had drifted in alone and friendless to ride for world honours and have them snatched from him by a single protest. But why think of that now? Somewhere in this crowd was Hugh Barrington, his friend . . . maybe Judy. His pulse quickened at thought of her.

Inquiry at round-up headquarters disclosed to him Hugh's hotel. He located it presently. The clerk nodded towards the bar-room. There he found Barrington.

He walked up to slap the big cowboy on the back. Hugh whirled, his eyes revealing no great pleasure.

"Howdy, Sage," he said thickly. "What you doing here?"

Grey was shocked at the change that had come over Barrington in the short time since they had parted. His face was pouchy, discoloured. And it was obvious that he had been drinking heavily. Something of a pang stabbed Grey. Not for Hugh, but for Judy.

"What you drinking?" Barrington asked, eyeing him with a strange coldness. "You're just up from the ranch?"

"Yes." He could have sworn Barrington started. "I've left the Cross Anchor."

Barrington's glass dropped from trembling fingers. It shattered on the bar. He mumbled an apology to the sour-faced bar-tender, who swiped up the trickling whisky.

"Left the Cross Anchor? Why? Where's Alice . . . is she . . . ?"

"Left her, too," grimly. "Just didn't fit."

"Couldn't take it." Hugh grinned. "Didn't think

216

you could. Fool play in the first place, if you'd ask me."

"Nobody's asking you," Grey snapped. "You once suggested we tie up in the wild string. I've got Widow-Maker with me."

"The hell you have! Got any money?"

"A thousand or so!"

"I'll sell you a half interest in my string for a thousand cash if you'll throw in Widow-Maker." Hugh was all attention now. "He'll make the string . . . give us about twenty head. I've picked up some Brahma steers and calves. Have another?" as Grey finished his drink.

"No thanks. Let's get our deal closed up." Grey moved away into the lobby.

"Be with you in a minute."

Hugh dashed off another drink before he followed. Grey looked round for Judy. He wanted to ask Hugh about her. But he dared not evince too great an interest. Besides, in going in with Hugh, he was determined to give Judy a wide berth. Mason had told him he had no right . . . in his heart he knew he hadn't.

The deal was quickly concluded and the partnership of Barrington and Sage formed. A lawyer summoned by the hotel clerk drew up a contract. They signed before a notary. Hugh threw in the rodeo contracts he had—one for a Wyoming fair following the Belle Fourche round-up and one for a big rodeo in Oregon.

The two shook hands. At the invitation of Barrington, Grey moved into the cowboy's hotel room. Still no mention of Judy. Apparently she had not yet arrived. He did not bring up the subject. After a time Hugh left him.

Grey went to the rodeo-grounds to look over the wild string. Good-looking horses, they were. And half of them were his. It gave him a comfortable feeling. Here was a real thrill, this being a partner in such a business. When they announced the famous Widow-Maker was in the string as a final horse, success was assured.

The following day saw the start of the three-day round-up. Hugh and Grey both entered the pitching contests. They made their rides to the plaudits of the thousands. After the show was over, Grey tended to the wild string. Then he ate supper alone in a little place down by the river, feeling smugly pleased with himself. That evening he hunted up Barrington—in a bar-room—from which Grey could not coax him.

It was well after midnight when Hugh came reeling into the room. Grey said no word. But Barrington wanted to talk. And, to Grey's disgust, he wanted to talk about Judy.

"She's going to leave me if I keep on drinking," he said in a maudlin, tearful mood. "Says she won't stand for it. Women are crazy. They don't know what they want. But I got round her. No woman can out-nigger me."

Grey persisted in his silence.

"I promised to let her go back into the rodeo if she'd stick. She'll be riding to-morrow. She's due in early in the morning." He started away.

"It's morning now," Grey said, singularly upset with the knowledge that he soon would be face to face with Judy. "Where are you going?"

"Forgot to have a drink on Judy coming back," Hugh grinned as he staggered out of the room.

It was almost daybreak when he returned. Grey helped him to bed.

"Be snoozin' when Judy gets here," he muttered. "You meet her like a good fellow, Sage. I'll be all right when I wake up."

Disgustedly, Grey dressed and went downstairs.

Inquiry revealed that the train would arrive in less than half an hour. Quitting the hotel, he strolled about waiting. For all his outward calm, he was far from easy inside. His heart was hammering. In a few moments now he would see Judy. But with each thought of her came another of Hugh, in a drunken stupor at the hotel. What had come over the big cowboy to start him drinking like this? Yet what difference did it make? If Barrington chose to drink himself to death, it was his own business. Certainly it was the affair of no one else . . . unless it was Judy.

The train rolled in, ground to a halt. With pounding pulse he edged out on the station platform, stood sweeping the throng that came belching forth from the coaches. Then presently he spotted Judy, a trim little figure alighting from a Pullman. He fought down a mad desire to rush to her, seize her in his arms, smother her with kisses. He managed to walk towards her slowly. She sighted him, dropped the bag the porter had handed out, flew to him. Before he knew it she was in his arms, their lips were clinging. She was muttering little inarticulate cries.

"Where's Hugh?" she asked breathlessly, pulling herself away.

"He worked late." Grey avoided her eyes. "Figured he'd be tired. He asked me to meet you."

"You're the poorest liar I ever knew, Grey Sage," she flashed. "Hugh is drinking, isn't he?"

"I'll carry your grip," he said. "Hungry?"

"I wasn't." She was biting back the tears. "But as long as Hugh is sleeping, if you care to—"

"Come on, then." He picked up her bag, took her by the arm. "Have a nice trip?"

"No." She pulled away from him, slipped her hand on to his arm, her fingers clutching him caressingly. "I'm a bit tired . . . and worried."

"Alice? Is she—"

"She is all right. She's flying East before long. Grey, you're going to give her a divorce, aren't you?"

"Why should I?"

"Because . . ." She stopped short. "I thought perhaps some day there might be . . ." She dropped his arm. "I guess Hugh being as I know he is has upset me. Let's not talk. It's hard for me to talk to you when I feel like I do, Grey."

"Ride or walk?" They had passed through the station.

"I'd rather check the bag and walk, if you don't mind."

"I'd like it. There's a little place across town, near the river, where we can eat a bite and be quiet."

She thanked him with her eyes. Checking the bag, they went outside in the early morning, walked briskly uptown.

In every direction from the little city stretched the prairies, their dun colour splashed with the red and brown and greys of clay banks. Sunlight reflected blindingly on scattered patches of alkali. The tang of sage was in the air. It brought Grey's shoulders back. His chest expanded with a deep breath.

"You love it, don't you, cowboy?" she asked quietly.

"Reckon I do. But it's making me hungry. Eat a bite now?"

"I . . . I guess so."

Then they were inside a neat little café. He had ordered. They sat looking at one another.

"A penny for your thoughts," she bantered with a brave attempt at gaiety.

"They aren't worth it." He smiled grimly. "But

the subject-matter is worth plenty—it's you."

"And what were you thinking of me?" He noticed that her gaze fell, that she had suddenly found something of interest on the table-cloth.

"I'm thinking I never loved any one before like I love you," he blurted out. "I'm thinking that it's hopeless . . . that I'll just go on loving you for ever and you'll never be any nearer . . . just a sort of an ideal I'll always worship."

When she looked up there were tears in her eyes.

"You're not very high yourself, cowboy. While there's life there's hope, you know. At least, it would be easier if—"

"If I would divorce Alice?" he finished for her. "Do you want me to, Judy?"

"Yes." Her voice had grown husky. "Then I'd know that even if you weren't mine, you wouldn't be anybody else's."

"But the grounds! I can't bring myself to ask a divorce on any grounds that would hurt Alice."

"You love her?" quickly, somewhat accusingly, he thought.

"No. But I don't think it's much of a man who will deliberately blacken a woman's character, do you?"

"I never thought of it that way."

"And besides, if I asked for a divorce now, they'd say it was money I was after. I don't want her money."

"It's a noble way to look at it, Grey." Her eyes kindled with a new light. "And I'm proud of you." She reached over, patted his hand that lay on the table. "The better I know you, the finer I think you are."

"That's all that means anything to me, Judy," soberly. "But it doesn't do us any good."

"Yes, it does. Love is one thing, love with respect is another. One can love many times, perhaps. But respect is the foundation of lasting love. If the world knew how deeply I love I'd be . . . they'd call me most everything. I'm married, yet I love—"

"Who?" He knew what she would say, but he waited breathlessly for her answer.

"You." Her gaze met his unflinchingly. "In my heart I don't feel that I am doing anything that wasn't intended for me to do . . . I don't feel there is any sin. Now can you see Alice's angle, Grey? She was engaged to Jay before she ever saw you. They had a spat. That's what has made Alice appear cold. She isn't, really. And she has a real affection for you, Grey. But not the depth one needs for marriage."

"Our cases are alike, I guess. You haven't done anything to be ashamed of. Neither has Alice. She deserves a divorce if we can just figure a way."

They fell silent while they ate. Nor did they make any further attempt at conversation until they had left the café.

"I suppose I'd better go to the hotel and rest up a little. I'm riding to-day."

"Please!" The plea burst from him. "It's too dangerous, Judy. Don't go back to it. For my sake."

"You old dear!" She caressed his arm. "You out there riding, revelling in the thrill of the thing, and still telling me that it is too dangerous. I was born on a horse, Grey. I've got it in me just like you have. I don't know anything else. Be a sport, cowboy. When I come out this afternoon I'll kick them both ways from Sunday just like you do."

"You won't change your mind—for me?" he asked, hurt.

"I'd do anything for you . . . almost." She was deadly serious. "But I've got to have something now, or I'll go crazy—got to have an outlet for these emotions that are stifling me. Please—ask anything but that, Grey."

"It will be a mighty nervous day for me, Judy," he said. "If anything should happen to you—"

"The same goes for you, cowboy," she put in softly. "Perhaps you think it's going to be fun for me watching you ride. Let's quit being babies. We are doing the thing we want to do more than anything else in the world. If one of us should . . . but we're not going to get hurt. We're going to live to be old white-haired folks and . . ."

"Be together," he said as they entered the hotel.

"I hope so," she breathed, squeezing his arm.

He went up first. Barrington was coming out of his stupor. With a quick drink as a bracer, Grey hurried him into his clothes, threw open the windows to air out the room. Then he went downstairs and brought Judy up, slipped away as the two greeted each other without affection.

Chapter XXII

They were behind the chutes, Barrington, Grey and Judy. She had made her ride aboard a savage bucker—a marvellous exhibition of horsemanship. Grey recognized in her a rider who could and would go far. And she seemed to love the thrill of it. She had come back from the arena laughing, her hair blowing in the breeze.

"Fine work," Grey had exclaimed admiringly, meeting her with outstretched hands. For a second they stood fingers clasped.

"Break!" Barrington exploded.

He whirled, left them abruptly. Judy flushed, pulled away. Grey paled. His lips set grimly. Barrington's single word, which carried a world of meaning, put him on his guard. Other annoying things had come up between them in the last few hours. He had overlooked them because Barrington was still drinking. Judy had appeared at the rodeo-field with eyes that looked suspiciously as though she had been crying.

"Hugh Barrington out of chute Number Four on High Dive!" The announcement broke in on them.

"Hugh can't ride to-day," Judy cried in affright. "We can't let him, Grey."

"How are we going to stop him?"

"He's been drinking. Please, Grey . . . try, won't you?"

He strode away. But with little hope of success. He came upon Barrington climbing the chutes.

"Hadn't you better call off the ride for to-day, Hugh?" he suggested. "You're not in shape."

"Who the hell says I'm not?" the big fellow demanded belligerently. "Keep your nose out of my affairs, Sage."

"Suit yourself." Grey shrugged. "But you're drunk, Hugh—so drunk you can't ride a sawbuck, let alone a bronc."

Hugh leaned down to an uncertain footing. "Who the hell says I'm drunk?" he roared. "I won't have you talking like that. Damn you, I've got just plenty to say to you on other things."

"Go sleep it off," Grey snorted. "You'll just make an ass of yourself if you climb aboard . . . get your neck kinked."

"They never did come too tough for me," Barrington boasted. "They never will. I only wish they'd give me Widow-Maker. Just to show you the brute can be ridden. I wouldn't quit him, even if he pitched into a fence, and collect a thousand dollars on a crooked clean-up, like another jasper I know."

Grey's lips whitened. His eyes were cold, laced with angry flame. The voice of Judy steadied him—as it had so many times before.

"You can't stop him," she whispered from his

elbow as Hugh whirled back, started mounting the chute. "You're just wasting your time . . . and taking abuse."

"Is that the way he talks to you?" he demanded.

She hung her head. Her silence was answer enough.

"This can't go on, Judy. We're leaving . . . I'll make him take over my interest. I won't put up with this."

"You would if you were married to him. You can go. But I . . . Can't you see your being here is all that makes things bearable? Promise me you won't leave?" She was pleading with him. He turned back to watch Barrington lowering himself unsteadily into the chute.

"I'll stay," he told her. "Run along now. I'll keep an eye on Hugh."

"Thanks." She disappeared behind the corrals.

Barrington came out on a vicious bucker, for all his drunkenness riding like a champion. But the brutality that liquor fired within him got the upper hand. He fell to abusing the horse, trying to gouge out an eye with his spinning rowels. The judges saw what he was about. Warnings were shouted. But Hugh had thrown caution to the wind, was howling like an Indian, riding like a madman.

"Drunk, ain't he—your pardner?" a cowboy observed to Grey.

Grey turned away to keep from answering.

"Trying to get an eye," the cowboy persisted. "Ain't that one of your own horses? Must be pretty expensive tied up with a walloper like that."

Grey moved out of earshot.

A great shout brought him about. In a frantic attempt to scratch the bronc high, Hugh Barrington had been thrown. One foot had caught in a stirrup. The horse was kicking at him savagely.

Pandemonium broke loose. Women were screaming, men shouting. Pick-up men were closing in. The arena became a blur of dust and deadly action. Judy appeared from nowhere, was clutching Grey's arm.

Then they had the bronc, had released Barrington's foot. He lay prone in the dirt of the arena. Interns ran up with a stretcher. A doctor appeared. Judy and Grey pushed through the crowd, followed to the farrier's tent. The doctor motioned them both outside.

Some time later he came forth.

"Is he . . ." Judy faltered.

"Just knocked out." The doctor smiled wanly. "He's coming to now. No bones broken, but a close shave. He'll be laid up for a few days with bruises and contusions. He'd better let the liquor alone if he's going to follow this game. I suppose you're Judy?"

"Yes."

"He's asking for you—and for Grey Sage."

They went in the tent, unconsciously hand-in-hand.

Hugh was stretched on a cot on his back staring up through pain-glazed eyes.

"The horse wasn't tough," he whispered brokenly. "I'd had more than I figured. I'll be all right. Forget it, will you?"

"Sure." Grey laid a hand on his shoulder.

Judy dropped to her knees beside him. "Try and rest. I'll line up a way to get you to the hotel."

Barrington closed his eyes wearily. When he did not open them they left the tent together. In silence they made their way into town—a sad-eyed speechless Judy who scarcely looked up; a Grey Sage sunk in thought that took scant notice of things about him.

Grey, with a doctor, went back. He found Barrington still asleep under the influence of an opiate. They loaded him in an ambulance, rolled him to the hotel, Grey at his side, a comforting hand on his arm. Once the big fellow was in bed in the hotel, Grey took his hat.

"I'll just be going now, Judy," he said. "I'll send a nurse to help you."

"I'll manage somehow. A rest will do him good."

"But if you ride to-morrow, you'll need rest too. I'll send a nurse. I'll stay in the lobby. If you need anything call me."

She followed him outside into the hall, offered her hand.

"Thank you, cowboy," she said softly. "I don't know what I'd do without you."

"I hope you never will," he said. "I'd just like to fit in always—somewhere."

"You will." He dropped her hand, drew her into his arms and kissed her. She made no resistance.

"Good-night, Judy," he whispered.

"Good-night . . . dear." She whirled and was gone.

The following day Barrington remained in bed. Grey Sage and Judy rode. Both won their events. His fear for her passed as he watched her. She was a horsewoman with few equals. And he found happiness in her success.

"Sage," the manager of the rodeo said, coming up to him behind the chutes. "There's a little matter we've got to straighten out. Meet with the committee tonight at headquarters."

"Anything wrong?" Grey demanded anxiously.

"We'll explain to-night." The official passed on.

"What do you suppose it is?" Grey asked Judy, who came up at the moment.

"I don't know," she said. "But . . . why try and cover up with you any longer, Grey? When Hugh is under the influence of liquor he'll do anything. There's probably something wrong with the contracts."

"Forget it," he said.

In silence they mounted and rode back to town. But Grey Sage was scarcely prepared for the thing when it did burst upon him. He faced the rodeo committee.

"It's your partner, Barrington." The chairman came directly to the point. "He's been throwing money around like a drunken sailor. Our merchants report he has got into them for several hundred dollars. I suppose you have ample funds to take care of such a thing? Unless you have, we cannot pay off until our merchants are satisfied."

"This is my first show with Barrington," Grey said. "How much do our contracts amount to?"

"We'll pay you in the neighbourhood of two thousand. But Barrington's bills alone amount to close to that much." He thumbed through a list of statements before him. "Our merchants report he has been drunk constantly. He rode yesterday under the influence of liquor, a thing strictly forbidden by our rules. We're looking to you to straighten him out—either that or he is barred from further competition. We're members of the National Association, which means he is barred from any Association show . . . as well as your string."

"We'll cover the bills as far as our contract money will go," Grey said. "I, personally will make up the balance . . . with day money, or what money I win."

He left the conference in a furious frame of mind. Barrington had wrecked the first chance they had had together. He could countenance no such deals. At least, he was honest. There seemed nothing to do but dissolve the partnership. He could probably split the string, eventually build one for himself.

Judy! She needed him more now than ever before. To leave her, to run away—as he had run away from other unpleasant situations—was to play the coward. Face it he must—face it and fight it.

For the first time he found himself wishing for money. Money would straighten the thing out so easily. But what little he possessed after buying in with Barrington had gone for feed-bills for the stock. There was no place he could turn. If he won the finals, his money and Judy's winnings would clean up the accounts.

Much as he dreaded it, he went in search of Judy. He found her in the hotel lobby, huddled in a chair, staring out to the street. He dropped down beside her.

"I hate like the devil to tell you this, Judy," he said, "but—"

"There's only one way for us to be pals," she encouraged him. "Come clean, cowboy. We can take it, can't we—together?"

Never before had he loved her as he did now. There was something so wholesomely good, so frank and honest about her. It gave him confidence. He blurted out the whole truth.

"That's just his look-out," she said when he

had finished. "You're not putting up a cent to pull him out of the hole—understand that."

"Half of this outfit belongs to me," he protested. "I've got to protect the horses to fill the other contracts. These jaspers wouldn't bat an eye at attaching the string."

"They might at that," she admitted. "But . . ."

"I know what you're going to say." He gazed at her fondly. "After all, there's no one I would rather help than him . . . for you."

"Thanks." She patted his arm. "I could wire Alice for a loan."

"You'll do nothing of the kind," he snapped out angrily, only to soften at the hurt look in her eyes. "I'm sorry," he apologized, "just the thought of having Alice . . ."

"I understand. First we've got to find out how deep we're in. Then we'll meet it . . . you and I, cowboy."

"We'll come out some way."

"There's no one else I could bring myself to owe . . . dear." She smiled wanly.

Chapter XXIII

Summer lengthened into autumn on the Wyoming prairie. A chill crept into the night air, but the heat of the day only seemed to increase. The breezes whining across the griddle-hot flats of cowland were like draughts from a furnace. Cattle huddled rump to rump, fighting flies that hovered in swarms over their backs. Cattle bunched about putrid water-holes, bellowing with thirst. But this year Grey Sage did not see it. For the first time in his life, he was away from this thing he hated above all else.

Both Judy and he had won the finals in bronc-riding at Belle Fourche. By pooling their winnings they had managed to pay off Hugh's indebtedness and clear their string. They had gone on to Andover to play the Wyoming fair. There, with a decent break, they had a chance to earn back the money they had lost.

Barrington promised anything. But once he was up and about, he quickly forgot his pledges. The first day of the Andover fair, he barged into the hotel weaving on his feet and became abusive.

Embarrassed to the point of shame, not so much for himself as for Judy, Grey hustled him away. Gone now was any mood to argue with the big cowboy. A cold hatred had settled down upon Grey. He was determined to take no more. When, presently, Barrington's maudlin talk swung around to Judy, Grey stopped him.

"Leave her out of it," he warned. "After she threw her winnings into the pot to pay your booze bills at Belle Fourche, I should think you'd have the decency to let her alone."

"Who the hell do you think you are, talking about my wife that way?" Barrington leered. "I'll say what I please. I'm no fool. And I'm not blind either." He was working himself into a frenzy. "I won't have it, damn you. She's my wife, do you hear?"

In an attempt to avoid an open break, Grey Sage held his tongue. He left abruptly, sought out Judy. They stood together in her room, looking down into the street.

"I can't go through with this any longer," he told her.

"I know it isn't pleasant for you," she said. "But . . . I have to take it. If we could only keep him away from drink. Did it ever strike you there is something worrying him—something that makes him like this? He never used to be."

"I have thought of it. He was not this way at the ranch."

"There he goes now," she whispered, edging back. "I wonder what he's up to."

Barrington had reeled out of the lobby to the street below.

Grey knew, but he said nothing. Liquor had become Barrington's consuming passion. Their pleas availed them nothing. Big Hugh would not or could not break off his drinking. A show-down was inevitable. But how to relieve Judy's suffering. She looked so tired of late. Dark circles had appeared beneath her eyes. It was plain she was worrying to the point of illness.

He left her after a time, quit the hotel and went out in the packed streets to wander aimlessly. Nor had he returned when Hugh came back. Judy, however, seeing Hugh approaching, fled to the room, where he followed her.

"We're moving," he announced thickly. "Damned Sage said to-day we had to cut expenses. Guess he's right. So we'll cut 'em. Hotel bills first. Mouthy devil that Sage. Tried to tell me what to do. I told him where to head in instead. I'll show him I can cut expenses. Bought a tent. We're going to live like other rodeo folks. These snobs give me a pain, anyway."

"You mean you . . . are going to live in a tent?" fearfully. "Out at the rodeo-grounds?"

"Plenty good enough. Close to our work. Won't have these damned hotel bills. Pack your duds."

Thankful for this respite from constant bickering, she packed hurriedly. A bell-boy helped them down. Barrington made a show of settling at the desk.

"Got a ten?" he demanded of Judy. "I'm a little short."

She flushed. He was for ever doing things like this of late. He knew she had nothing—that it had taken every cent to settle his accounts in Belle Fourche.

"My partner will settle it," Barrington told the clerk. "Put it on Sage's bill."

Cheeks flaming with humiliation, Judy walked from the hotel with Barrington reeling along behind. Her heart was filled with boiling anger, not only at this man who was her husband, but also at Grey, who she knew, because of her, would settle the account.

She couldn't go through with it much longer. She hated Hugh Barrington—hated him as she never before had hated any other human being. Grey had been wonderful. But why didn't he do something? Why did he let this continue?

Thankful for the lowering light of evening, she entered the cab Hugh signalled, the while he explained thickly that their equipment had already been delivered. Once inside he fell asleep. She sat on the edge of the seat, aware of nothing about her, her heart and mind torn with savage, rebel-lious emotions.

No longer could she feel loyalty for this man beside her. She wanted Grey Sage. Yet she couldn't bring herself to go to him, seek the comforting protection of his arms, until she had broken clean with Hugh. But how could she break with Barrington? It was fear that held her—stark, terrible fear that tormented her by day, wakened her in cold perspiration at night.

The cab stopped at the rodeo-grounds. Without a word she alighted. Barrington came to with a start. He lurched out. Paying the driver from a scant supply of change, he reeled away to claim the tent and other equipage that had been delivered, carried it on his shoulders off a distance and pitched it. She made no effort to help him as he cursed and sweated at the task. When, presently, he had erected it he came over to her.

"There's your new home," he snarled. "I'll show that damned Sage I can cut expenses. You'll take it and like it."

"What has come over you, Hugh?" she pleaded. "You didn't used to be this way. Won't you tell me?"

Once as he stared she caught a glimpse of the old Hugh. He was on the point of telling her something. Instantly the cold light flared into his eyes.

"Nothing the matter with me," he growled. "That's just another one of your crazy ideas—yours and that Sage. I hate that jasper."

"I guess it's mutual," she flashed before she thought. "But you've got to admit he's played fair with you."

"I'm not so sure. I moved you out here to get you away from him. He thought I listened to his big talk on cutting expenses. But I didn't. I just out-niggered him. And I don't ever want to catch him around here. You understand?"

He seized hold of her wrist, twisted it painfully.

"Hugh," she cried in terror. "Whatever has come over you?"

"I'm not so dumb," he said brutally. "I don't want that Sage around you any more."

He cast her aside roughly, strode away. She stood watching him until he had disappeared. It seemed the end of everything. Why did she stay? Why did she stand this abuse?

She went inside the tent presently to throw herself on a cot and cry herself to sleep.

The Andover fair concluded, with a profit of a few hundred dollars, which Hugh was sober enough to receive and divide, they moved on to the U-Bar rodeo. Again, as at Belle Fourche, Grey and Judy had won in the finals. But they took their success in silence. Once on the road, it was Barrington who celebrated it by getting uproariously drunk.

They had made camp at U-Bar. Barrington had staggered in the tent beyond the rodeo-grounds. He threw himself on a cot. Once he was asleep, Judy had stolen out. She had encountered Grey near the corrals. "He's threatened you if you ever come near," she sobbed. "Grey . . . I guess you'd better leave."

"I'll leave when you go with me," he said stubbornly. "The only reason I'm staying is you. I hate Barrington. But until you begin to talk sense—"

"What's come over us all?" she cried. "We had such hopes, such plans . . . look at the way things have turned out."

"Do you love Hugh?" he demanded.

"No!"

"Is it loyalty?"

"Anything I may have felt for him once is dead."

"Then why don't you . . . Judy, why are you breaking both our hearts?"

"I'm afraid, Grey," she murmured, finding her way into his waiting arms. "Terrified day and night—that's the only reason I'm staying. Won't you please go? Some time perhaps we can . . . when you get your divorce. I heard from Alice to-day. She's packing to fly East. She sent her regards."

"I'm not interested in Alice. It's you, Judy. Why will you go on letting us eat our hearts out?"

"Because I'm afraid. Please, Grey, go. Later, perhaps . . ."

"All right, if that's the way you feel about it," he said abruptly. "But I thought that you loved me."

"Do you doubt it? Have you ever doubted it?

The thing will work out—if we're careful. Until that time—"

"I suppose it's good-bye?"

She regarded him with a stunned look.

"I guess it is." Tears sprang to her eyes.

He whirled, strode away angrily.

But Grey Sage did not go. Neither did he attempt to see Judy alone—partly through anger, partly because of a deliberate resolve to force her to her senses.

Came a day when he saw Barrington swing on his horse and strike out towards town. He could stand it no longer. So he loped over to the tent behind the feedlots. His nerves tingled with the unfriendliness of the place. There was no sign of life about—only the tent glaring white against the Wyoming mountains, sharp-etched by the blasting sun.

He rowelled his snorting pony up to the tent, dismounted. The flap swung back.

"I thought maybe . . ."

He stopped blankly to stare, the speech he had planned to open the conversation fled. He suddenly found it difficult to talk to Judy. There was a barrier between them—a barrier he himself had raised in his mind. She was confronting him now, the woman he loved. She wore a trim, starched house-dress that made her look even younger and prettier. Her skin was smooth as agate, tanned, glowing with colour.

"I didn't come . . . to embarrass you," he managed to blurt out. "I just had to come."

"You shouldn't have, Grey." He was conscious of her shrinking. "Hugh is so savage in his hatred. You . . . we have to be careful."

She surveyed him with eyes in which she could not conceal the love. Warned by a sense of insecurity, but drawn on by a crazy notion to find out once and for all whether hope must be abandoned, he forced himself to stand his ground.

"I wouldn't have come but . . . hot, isn't it?" He squatted on his rowels in the shade of the tent, cursed himself for his inability to voice the thoughts cascading through his mind. "You can't stay holed up like this, Judy," he blurted out. "You've just got to do something."

"There's nothing I can do," desperately. "Grey, must we go into all that again?"

"Let's put an end to this thing that is eating out both our hearts. Tell me what you want me to do."

"I don't know," she admitted. "I only know that Hugh will kill you if he gets a chance. He's afraid you'll leave him with the string . . . afraid that I'll . . . he's warned me time and again, Grey. I'd go with you if we had the right. But we are both married. Please don't make it any harder. I'm living in mortal terror now."

"And I don't propose to let you." He leaped up.

Before she could protest he had gathered her in his arms. She settled there with a contented sigh.

"I wish you'd make me do things, Grey," she whispered. "But I'm so afraid . . . I just can't go on like this much longer."

"Leave him," he urged. "Go back—"

"Where? Alice has probably left for the East by now. There is no place to go! Here, at least, I can see you at a distance."

"So that's it?" he said exultingly. "You're staying just to . . . see me once in awhile?"

She nodded, but she did not look up.

"All right, then." He released her suddenly. "I'm going to file for divorce from Alice. Then we'll get a stake. It won't take long. We're the best riders in the game. We could go to the top together."

"I know, dear. But the way you are tied up with Hugh, it will mean sacrificing everything. You can't just pull out and take your share of the string. You can't—"

"Can't leave you," he finished for her. "You're right. It's a mess, Judy—another of the messes I always seem to be getting into."

"There'll be a way. I know there will. But you'd better go now. Hugh might come back." She pulled away from him, was staring off towards town. "Grey!"—a wild, stifled cry—"there he comes."

Grey Sage whirled. Barrington had suddenly

ridden out from behind the chutes, was loping towards the tent. The set expression on his pouchy face revealed nothing. But the way he rode, gouging his mount with the rowels, was evidence of the ugly mood he was in.

Grey stood motionless until the big cowboy had jerked up beside him.

"Caught you, huh?" Barrington lashed out. "Figured I would."

He swung down, swaggered over to Grey, stood spread-legged before him. And, Grey noted swiftly, he was wearing a forty-five.

"You get the hell away from here and stay. Do you understand?"

Barrington's hand dropped down to his cartridge-belt. He fingered the butt of the gun. But it was not the Barrington of old: it was a new Barrington, shifty-eyed, uneasy.

Grey sized him up from the tips of his sloppy boots to the tie askew at his throat. Barrington had always been so neat before. But of late he was unkempt, dishevelled, seemed to have lost all hold.

Grey dared a glance at Judy. There was terror in her eyes. And she was holding her handkerchief to her lips—a gesture he remembered from the first day he had seen her at the chutes in Arapahoe.

Then he was speaking—speaking in a voice that crackled.

"I'm leaving . . . leaving your whole damned

layout. I've got my fill of your breed, Barrington. I'm sorry I ever tied up with you. But it was my own fault. I went into it with my eyes open, although I was plenty fooled by the big front you put on. I'm through now. And I'm demanding half of the string."

"I'm not splitting the string," Barrington snarled. "You'll stay, or you'll get out without a thin dime. But if you do stay, you're keeping away from my wife."

Utter contempt replaced the first flush of anger that surged through Grey. His fists balled. He took a step forward. Instead of whipping out the gun, Barrington leaped back.

Grey shrugged.

"I thought so, you damned coward—thought that gun was just a bluff, like all the rest of you. You haven't got the guts to use it when a man is facing you." He secured his mount, swung in the saddle. "You've made your play. I'm calling your hand. It's a showdown, jasper, from this day on. You're going to listen to something else besides that whisky-soaked brain of yours for a change.

"I didn't mean to cause you any embarrassment, Judy. If you can get it through this walloper's head, try and . . ." He stopped. "Don't tell him anything. Barrington, if I ever hear of another word of abuse towards Judy, if you ever lay a hand on her, I'll kill you."

The face she turned up to him was glowing. But the fear in her eyes sealed her lips.

He lifted his horse in a gravel-flinging lunge, rode away without so much as a backward glance. In his heart, too, was cold fear—not of Barrington, who only stood weaving on his feet and staring after him, but for Judy, the woman he loved. In the blazing anger of the moment he was determined to have an end to the thing.

Riding to town, he stopped at the first sign bearing the name of an attorney. Swinging down, he tied his horse, went inside. The lawyer scanned his contract. The advice he gave was terse, pointed. Stick or lose everything. Borrowing a pencil and paper Grey dashed off a letter to Barrington, turning over all his rights to the string, including Widow-Maker. Placing the note with the cancelled contract in an envelope supplied by the dumb-founded lawyer, he addressed it. Going back to his horse, he rode down the street towards the post-office. At least now he could get away from it all. He drew rein, a lead weight on his heart.

"Running away from yourself." Of a sudden he seemed again to hear the words of Alice—a cool, musical voice that sometimes he had loved, sometimes hated. "Running away from your own fear . . . from Judy . . . from people."

He had protested then, was protesting now to himself. But within him he knew she had spoken the truth. He was running away—running away from Barrington. Not through fear—even yet he didn't know the meaning of fear. But he was running away from trouble, from unpleasantness he could not force himself to face, from the one thing he loved above all else—Hugh Barrington's wife.

"That's what he wants me to do—give him the string and clear out," he growled under his breath. He reined about, rowelled back up the street. "Running away, am I?" he demanded aloud of the pony, which laid an ear back against its head. "I'll show him . . . I'll show the world Grey Sage isn't running away from anything."

He felt better for the decision. It meant that again he would be near Judy, even though their meetings would be indefinite and far between.

Chapter XXIV

High up in the Rockies, frost-nipped aspen splashed the sombre green of pine with vivid colour. Timberline was brown, barren, lifeless. Winter would presently turn those mountains to infernos of bitter cold and snarling storms. A rawness crept into the air: a rawness that added to the charm of Indian summer—gorgeous, hazy days when the mountains were but a faint blue on the horizon, unreal and ever-changing.

Always on the look-out for a word with Judy, Grey Sage waited in vain. For big Hugh, openly hostile now, seemed ever in attendance. A smile, a glance filled with meaning, was Grey's only reward. Occasionally their hands touched as they passed near the chutes of some rodeo. For she was riding—riding in a way that was carrying her swiftly to a world championship. And though Barrington did not know it, Grey always inspected her saddle-rigging before she came out.

After the affair at U-Bar he had stayed with the string. The fame of Widow-Maker spread. Their horses were in demand at every rodeo. But Grey had left things entirely up to Barrington. He had thrown himself into the arena events to occupy his mind. The violent moods that possessed him found an outlet in reckless riding.

He went in for bronc-riding, roping, bull-dogging. His Association points piled up until not only the bronc-riding championship but the title of world-champion cowboy was within his grasp.

Many times he had been on the verge of pulling out, letting the entire thing go, convinced that none of it was worth while. Yet, try as he would he could not bring himself to leave Judy. He loved her, pitied her, condemned her, all in the same breath. He thrilled to her superb riding and poise in the saddle. Time and again in the passing weeks he had been on the point of attempting to persuade her to go away with him. He never did. He knew beforehand what her answer would be.

He had heard nothing from Alice. Neither had he taken any steps to secure a divorce. As time went on, he saw less and less reason why he should obtain that divorce. Apparently Judy was lost to him. A divorce would gain him nothing. And he found a secret satisfaction—a gloating, unhealthy satisfaction—in denying legally to Mortimer the happiness of which he himself had been cheated.

The constant state of mental turmoil he endured made him bitter, cynical—left him looking out upon the world through eyes suspicious of everything, eyes ever alert for he did not know what. From Pendleton to Calgary and down to Salinas they went, the hard-riding Grey Sage sharing honours with the vicious Widow-Maker. The men in the arena, once chummy, began to avoid him. His method of riding became dangerously spectacular, reckless to a degree that kept the onlookers gasping for breath, cheering hysteri-cally. He seemed to have lost all control of himself in his savage determination to win the Association championship whatever the cost.

Came the Arvada Stock Show, the last Association point show of the season. Winter—bitter, savage winter that swooped down from the towering Rockies—lashed the city with arctic fury. Frozen snow crunched on the pavements. The bells of the street cars, running to the stockyards stadium, clanged coldly, hollowly—bull's-eyes pierced the swirling snow with ghostly faintness.

Grey Sage drew Widow-Maker that night; in spite of the drunken Barrington, Grey had managed to keep the drawings straight. Society night at the Stock Show! The boxes at the stadium gleamed with jewels and costly wraps. Expensively gowned women screamed them-selves hoarse as white-faced men fought vicious broncs in the arena. The noise, the cheers, the bands drove the outlaws to a frenzy. For all the gaiety the air was surcharged with tension—a tension almost tangible that clutched men's throats, chilled their hearts and turned bad horses into tornados of fury.

Staring down the taut, bowed neck of Widow-Maker again, Grey Sage was more than ever aware of that tenseness. He gave no outward sign. But the whole thing set his nerves on edge, left them jumpy—never a good thing for a bronc-rider. Twice before he had looked down across those plastered ears of Widow-Maker.

How much had happened since the first time he had come out aboard the savage bronc at Arapahoe! He had just missed a championship then, due to Harmon's protest. But that had been a mythical, empty honour—a local award. Now he was after a real championship. And there was no Harmon to protest. Damn him! He was dead now—murdered. He hadn't thought of it for ages, it seemed.

Now he had the championship cinched, if he used a little caution. His points had piled up amazingly. True, he hadn't done so well at Pendleton, had lost ground, and had barely ridden into the finals. Not because he was thrown, but he was riding too recklessly, with too much abandon—riding with too little thought of safety. The wild pitching of the horses seemed to soothe the fury that seethed up within him, to goad him to action. He cared for nothing save to ride his horse in the most spectacular manner, now scratching as high as he could behind the ears, now tearing leather from the cantle-board of his own saddle.

It was a new Grey Sage—a man of fierce emotions he himself did not understand, always with spring-tight nerves ready to snap at the least provocation, determined to attain the goal of which he had been cheated, if he died in the attempt.

And now, for the third time, he sat close-penned aboard Widow-Maker—the horse that he, of all the bronc-riders in the game, had ridden.

Even this knowledge gave him little satisfaction. That the brute beneath him had almost killed him in the wire at the Cross Anchor, had injured other crack riders, meant nothing. This horse had caused all of his trouble. But for this particular horse, he would never have encountered John Harmon, would never have been dragged through a law court charged with murder. But for this horse he would never have been chief wrangler at the Cross Anchor, would never have married Alice.

That was all ended now—a closed chapter in his life—closed, he feared, like the chapter dealing with his greatest love, Judy.

He scarcely ever saw her now and, reluctant to cause her more suffering, had made few attempts to see her. What she must be enduring for the sake of her loyalty to Hugh pained him when he would allow himself to think of it.

After the fall at Belle Fourche, Barrington had quit riding. He had taken over the direction of the arena. And while, to all appearances, he was making an excellent arena director, Grey many times knew that the cowboy was dead drunk—a thing that increased his brutality to man and beast.

He jerked himself back. Beneath him was the mightiest of broncs—the horse that no other man could ride. Came to him a flash of wonder at just how Widow-Maker had been thrown into the open list. Hitherto the brute had always been held as a final horse. But here he was. And he, Grey Sage, was almost the first rider to be catapulted out of the chutes. Some of Barrington's direction, perhaps. What difference did it make? Yet it struck him as strange, that he, of all the others, should draw this particular horse.

For a moment his eyes moved away from the bronc beneath him. The regular mugger handling the gate was gone. In his place was Hugh Barrington. There was something ugly in his eyes—a look he could not fathom, a vague incomprehensible something that jerked Grey's nerves even tighter. There was nothing to do about it now. The supreme test of his career lay just ahead. He could win or lose the championship out there in that arena—out there aboard the toughest of all horses—an outlaw that brought crowds up screaming at every rodeo in the country.

He had got the feel of his saddle, tested his stirrups. He put his entire weight upon them, somehow suspicious that they might have been tampered with. The leather did not give. Apparently everything was all right.

He had fingered up the halter-rope. Widow-Maker was set for that first lunge, belly almost touching the ground, head cocked ready to pop forth like a cannonball.

"Let me have him, Hugh," Grey said in a coldly determined voice.

Barrington swung the gate. Widow-Maker lurched through, a half-ton of hell and brawn, to hit the hard-packed tanbark like a stone-crusher in front, double-barrelled, deadly behind.

Fame, success, the championship for which he had tried so gamely drummed in the brute's hoofs. A shudder of pain racked Grey Sage. Widow-Maker had not cleared the gate. Again, as at Arapahoe, the heavy barrier had struck him a terrific blow on the leg as he lunged past. The thing was so strangely a repetition of that other ride!

Suddenly he remembered. Hugh Barrington had been beside the gate at Arapahoe. There he had caught his first glimpse of Judy. Hugh had been his competitor for top honours then. His hurt leg had cost him that championship.

Fame and success were fading, replaced by fear—a nightmare of breathless, horrible fear. Pain stabbed at his leg, worked swiftly into his groin. Pain whipped the colour from his face.

"Is that jasper riding?" he heard a mugger breathe to Hugh Barrington. "To-night piles up his final points. A world champion! The best we've had in years. God A'mighty! He's hurt. Look at his face. He's suffering like hell."

The hostler stopped suddenly, conscious that he was talking to himself. From the corner of his eye Grey could see that Hugh had disappeared.

Out in the arena Grey Sage knew excruciating agony—bone-crushing, flesh-rending agony that only a bronc-rider aboard a savage outlaw knows. Widow-Maker uncorked new tricks. He spun like a top, sun-fished, swapped ends, went down across the tanbark pitching sky-high, curving his belly up to the floodlights, lighting end for end. His foghorn bellow beat back from the stadium walls, lined with white-faced spectators. Widow-Maker was giving an exhibition of pitching that stunned rather than set the crowd to cheering.

Of a sudden the pain in Grey's leg became unbearable . . . like it had at Arapahoe. The world came crashing down upon him. Again championship or defeat lay in the next lunge. He strained for the pick-up gun, praying that it would bring relief from the torment he was enduring, realizing that unless it came quickly, he never could hold out.

Then his leg was dead, numb, useless. One stirrup went flapping to goad the outlaw to greater fury. With it went his hope of victory—

hope for the championship. He found himself cursing Hugh Barrington; cursing him savagely, bitterly. A violent lurch fogged his brain. From somewhere out of space came a salvo of cheers. Boxes upheaved with glittering *ensemble.* Then the stadium itself went to pitching crazily. Thousands of faces ran together in blurred and jagged lines. Screams beat on his consciousness, dwindled away to utter silence. He was hurtling through space. Arc-lights looked like twinkling stars zooming down to meet him. He struck the ground with a terrific impact. Through eyes that registered, but in which there seemed no sight, he could make out the bawling outlaw directly above him. Great ripping hoofs came down. With his last ounce of strength he tried to roll to safety. A stunning pain tore through his chest. He was aware of the crunch of bones . . . his own bones. Comforting blackness rolled up like clouds to overwhelm him.

On a cot far back in the stadium Grey Sage's consciousness swung back through the emptiness of vast space. He opened eyes glazed with pain. The air reeked with the odour of anaesthetics. Sober-faced bronc-peelers were grouped about, noisy in their attempts at quiet in high-heeled boots and jangling rowels.

"The gate hit me as I came out . . ." came gaspingly from Grey's bloodless lips. "Hugh

Barrington . . . didn't swing it wide enough. It was him hurt me at Arapahoe. Damn him! He cost me . . . I'll get him, if it is the last thing I ever do. Did I break—"

"Be quiet," a grim-faced doctor commanded.

"But will I be able to . . . ride?"

The answer was lost. The stifling blackness of insensibility again overwhelmed the pain-racked Grey.

Chapter XXV

Hissing wind pelted snow against the frosted panes of a second-rate hotel in Arvada; snow drove along the street, whirled up to dim the lights that pierced the storm like pencilled beams. The wind was bitterly cold—crackly cold as the frozen blanket underfoot.

Beside a clanking radiator in a tiny room, Judy Barrington, wrapped in a coat, faced big Hugh.

"But I'm going to keep on riding," she cried desperately. "I'm going to be the champion, I tell you."

Hugh, weaving drunkenly in a chair, lifted bloodshot eyes of flint.

"And I'll see you dead first," he snarled. "You know the heartaches of this game . . . the blasted lives . . . the danger in those treacherous hoofs. It wouldn't be so bad if they meant certain death. But they only cripple and maim."

"I'm going to win the championship just the same. Maybe in it there will be some happiness. This . . . I can't stand it any longer. I've stuck to you, ruined my own life—for what? You've promised, you've lied."

"Once a bronc-rider always a bronc-rider," he said thickly. "It's in the blood. You ride until you get too old or get scared of the horses . . . or until some outlaw makes a cripple out of you, like that one danged near did me in Belle Fourche. Cripples you . . . do you hear, Judy? Damn it . . . you . . . he can't have you."

"Who can't have me?" His tone terrified the girl.

"You know—Grey Sage. He's the rodeo to you. He's all you ever think of. But he'll never have you."

"Hugh . . . you haven't . . . you wouldn't. No! no! Even you couldn't sink that low." She was wild with fear, jerking at his arm.

"He can't have you," he shouted crazily. "There's nothing left for me but you. I've made a mess of everything. I've . . . God, how I've loved you! I saw you slipping away from me. This Sage . . . Judy . . . Judy . . ." He buried his face in his hands, a forlorn figure—a big man giving way to tears.

Her hand moved to his sagging shoulder.

"Buck up, Hugh," she said wearily. "I've stuck with you even though it broke my heart, simply because I said 'I do.' You've wrecked your life and wrecked mine. But still I'm loyal. I've always been loyal. I want you to know that. Even though I love Grey Sage, I am the same woman that pledged her troth to you. You believe me?"

He stared up at her, eyes misty with tears.

"I know," he muttered brokenly. "And now, I'm asking you to try again. I can still make you happy. If I can't I'll give you a decent divorce. Give me one more chance?"

"What is it you want me to do now?" Her tone was hopelessly dead.

"Drift along with me through the rodeos next spring. By then, if I haven't proved I can snap out of it, if I can't let liquor alone, you can have your divorce. God knows you've got plenty of grounds. You've been a real sport. I'll sign a paper now. You can go on riding. I'll teach you a few new tricks. By summer you'll win your world championship. After that, if we haven't made the rifle . . ." His eyes were pathetic in their misery.

"You'll coach me . . . and not forbid me to ride?" Her mood changed. "It's a go, Hugh." The haunted light flared back into her eyes. "It's going to be so hard, though. You can't realize what it means. Just staying here to-night because you demanded . . . not seeing Grey ride. I've seen him the other two times he rode Widow-Maker. I seem to feel somehow that he needs me now. It's not the rodeo, it's him you hate, because he tried to help you against yourself. If you just knew of the things he did when you were . . . drunk." She squared her shoulders defiantly. "I'll stick with you until summer, provided you'll brace up and help me win my championship."

"Thanks, Judy." His whisper was hoarse. "I won't ask any more. I've got a little money—"

"Part of it is Grey's," accusingly.

"To hell with him!" A cold gleam shot his eyes. "Forgive me," quickly. "I'll leave his share with the Stock Show management. I've always paid him, haven't I?"

"We've always paid," she corrected.

He glanced at her—an inscrutable look.

"The new foreman up at the Cross Anchor was out to the stock yards to-day trying to sell me the rest of Harmon's wild horses, still good brutes."

"That's where you got your horses to start with," she said without interest.

Again he glanced at her—a look she could not fathom.

"Who said it wasn't?" he demanded.

She stared at him in surprise.

"Why, nobody." She shrugged, a resigned gesture of hopelessness. "Let it pass. What were you saying?"

"These horses are dirt cheap. I'll buy them to increase the string. Then I've got a homestead filing out beyond the Cross Anchor in the mountains. Not much of a house. But it will do for the winter. I'll coach you. Next summer . . . will you really give me one more chance, Judy?"

She faced him bravely, although her lips trembled.

"I will on one condition," she bargained. "And that is if by summer you haven't made good, you'll step out of the picture and let me marry Grey Sage."

"If he's divorced, you can," he sneered. But he

offered his hand, a great gnarled hand that trembled.

She noticed it. A flush of repulsion spread over her face. She took it with cold fingers.

"It's a bargain," he said. "I'll see this foreman yet to-night and buy the string." He rose uncertainly. "Roll in and rest. I'll be late."

After he had left the room, she threw herself on one of the twin beds. For an infinity of time she lay listening to the wind howling outside. From below drifted the muffled clang of street-cars, the occasional frosty chug of a motor. Then gradually the city grew quiet. Still she lay awake dreaming of Grey Sage.

It was daylight when Hugh came into the lobby of the hotel, stamping the snow from his boots. He went directly to the room.

"I bought that string from the Cross Anchor," he told her. "That leaves us a little money to run on. We can build up the homestead. You might spend some time with Alice while I'm getting it fixed."

"Spend some time with Alice now?" she said scornfully. "Do you think I'd throw myself on a friend for mercy?"

"What's wrong with you?" he demanded.

"Nothing," wearily, "only my self-respect is gone. Your actions have become the talk of the rodeo country. I'm branded, Hugh Barrington . . . branded, do you hear? . . . branded as the wife of a drunken rodeo promoter and crook."

Big Hugh winced under her scorn. But he managed to hold his tongue.

"We'd better have a bite and get going," he said presently in an attempt at a light tone. "I've made arrangements to winter the string at the Cross Anchor. By the way, Alice hasn't gone East yet. She sent an invitation by the foreman for you to visit her for a while."

Alice . . . the Cross Anchor! The words echoed hollowly in Judy's heart. She shivered as she dressed.

Downstairs presently she made a brave stab at breakfast. But she choked on the food. Half consciously she heard a newsboy crying an extra. "Morning Extra . . . Arapahoe Bulletin!" Something about the Stock Show. She couldn't catch it. But anyway, her mind was far away with Grey Sage.

Chapter XXVI

The sun rising in vivid colour over the rim of the frosty mountains reflected blindingly on endless miles of snow. Grey Sage awoke to conscious-ness, stared up into the haggard face of one of the arena muggers.

Through the night he had tossed deliriously. The mugger, who had volunteered to remain, had held him in bed. Two names were always on his lips—Hugh Barrington and Judy.

"Cowboy," Grey whispered huskily, when he was able to wrench his mind from the numbing pain in his shoulders and legs, "has . . . anybody . . . did Judy . . ." The hope in his gaze turned the mugger away.

"She hasn't heard yet," he muttered.

A quick hurt flashed in Grey's eyes.

"It was Barrington, damn him. It wasn't any accident. And he did it before at Arapahoe. He did this to keep me from . . . I'll . . ." The thin voice grew weaker. "Am I badly busted up?"

"Collar-bones, both legs, a hip."

"Will I ride again?"

"You've got to rest." The cowboy tried to change the subject.

"Rest, hell! Did Judy ride last night?"

"No. Nor Barrington didn't show up after. I

heard this morning he'd pulled his freight . . . made arrangements for the string to be shipped to the Cross Anchor to winter. He's probably going back there and hole up now that Harmon is out of the way."

The growing pain in Grey's eyes brought the cowboy closer.

"I reckon I know now what you're thinking, jasper," he said. "But . . . if she was to walk out on him, it would mean a murder and a suicide. Barrington is the meanest man I ever knew. And now he's done this. We knew around the chutes the minute he asked to swing that gate. He asked in Arapahoe too—when he was riding against you for top money. We didn't get wise to him then. But now we know. I tried to get that gate open. But he held it—damn his soul!—just enough so you'd get busted. Barrington hates your guts. He tried to kill you."

"I've never hurt him," Grey said.

"Only in his own booze-warped mind," the cowboy exploded. "It's the talk of the rodeo circuit—has been ever since you and—"

"Don't say it," Grey murmured wearily. "It's a damn lie. You tell them all so for me . . . until I'm able to tell them myself."

Winter dragged to a snarling end in the Rockies; grey days filled with twisting snow and screaming wind; dismal days when a wan sun played hide-

and-seek behind clouds that skimmed the helm of frostbitten pine and sage; days bitterly cold when a heatless sun glared down on desolate, snow-wrapped wastes that ran blindingly into a pearl-grey horizon.

Through long, dreary weeks Grey Sage lay on a hospital cot. Gradually youth left his eyes in which burned a cold, hard glint. His smouldering hatred for Hugh Barrington increased until it consumed him, turned his soul to ice.

After an infinity of time he was able to sit up, a shadow of his former self, face pallid and drawn, wrinkles webbing his eyes—wrinkles of suffering.

Finally he was allowed to walk—painful, halting steps. But in his heart burned a determination to win out against injuries that would have killed less hardy men. That and a cruel, heartless resolve to live, that he might run down Hugh Barrington and choke the life out of him. These two things finally sent him from the hospital with barely a limp. As he left, the doctor's admonition rang in his ears:

"Don't ever try to ride again, my boy. You'll be fit for a good many more years unless you crack up again. That leg will never clamp down on an outlaw. There's a kidney torn loose. Another spill would be too much for you."

Never ride again! Why, it was his life, all he knew—all he had ever known. And, for all the failure at the Arvada Stock Show, his nerve remained unshaken. For the moment he wished he had not survived. Then he thought of Barrington.

"Don't every try to ride again!"

It rang in his ears, became a haunting, tormenting warning. Doctor's bills paid, he had less than a hundred dollars. He had no work, nothing to which he could turn his hand. He could go back to the homestead on the Cheyenne river, back with old Mason. He revolted at that thought. Go back a failure! He'd die first, after the faith the old fellow had imposed in him. Perhaps he could rejoin the rodeo as a hostler. Thought of Barrington sickened him. Stark reality stared him in the face. Vengeance cried in his heart.

In the weeks he had lain in the hospital he had had no word of Barrington nor of Judy. A mental picture of her kept his mind in a turmoil. She had not cared enough to inquire concerning him. For months he had waited for word from her— word that never came. Evidently she had been playing with him, had forgotten once he was out of the picture. Yet he had held her in his arms. Her kisses had been warm, sincere.

The business of making a living cut short his bitter retrospection. Two things he must do: find work and locate Hugh Barrington.

But he found no work. The wild-horse strings had either put into ranches for the winter or had moved south along the border to the sunshine States for the annual cowboy contests. In a short time now they would be back, those rodeo-folk, starting down the hell-for-leather circuit. Soon would come Arapahoe. At Arapahoe but a few short months before he had just missed the championship, had set crowds wild with his spectacular riding.

A desperate resolve formed in his mind. He would take one more fling at the game. It was a gamble. If he lost . . .

"Don't ever try to ride again, my boy!" beat horribly on his ears.

Winter gave way to spring—a dreary, sodden spring of bleak grey skies. Patches of dirty snow fringed the brush. Muddy water trickled in rivulets across sagebrush flats that presently would crack and curl beneath a blasting summer sun. Water-holes were filled to overflowing, their gumbo rims death-traps for thirsty cattle. Frozen grass greened slowly. With heart-breaking slowness prairie-land took a new lease on life.

Far different from the man of a year before, Grey Sage rolled into Arapahoe. Then he had come out of the heart of cowland vibrating with vigour and vitality, secure in his own strength, timid yet confident of his ability to master the worst outlaws of the arena. Now his confidence was shaky, his heart heavy. Actual want goaded him on. Slow-burning hatred of Hugh Barrington warped his soul.

It was at the rodeo headquarters. He had gone there to contact Brown, whom he had not seen since the night he had been a bridegroom in the home of the secretary. That seemed ages ago. It had been his idea to question Brown about Barrington. Judy didn't matter now. The pain of her silent departure had become a numbness. He wanted Barrington—wanted to take up his trail, run him down, choke him to death.

But in the rodeo headquarters he came face to face with Judy. She started up at sight of him, advanced shyly, black-ringed eyes sad, pitiful, her whole attitude one of utter dejection.

"Judy!" burst from his whitened lips. He steeled himself quickly. "Where's Hugh?"

"Grey!" His name was almost a moan on her lips. "Grey!" Regardless of the few who turned to stare, she rushed forward, arms outstretched. "Oh, Grey, I've tried to find you. Where have you been?"

He avoided her, refused to meet her pleading gaze. "Guess it wouldn't have been very hard to find me—if you'd tried."

"What do you mean?" Her arms fell. She recoiled, face bloodless.

"Barrington knew where I was."

"Hugh knew?" She seized him by the arm. "He said . . . Grey . . . you look so pale. Are you sick?"

"Been in the hospital in Arvada since the Stock Show. Hugh . . ." It was on his tongue to tell her. Something held him back.

"Grey!" Tears welled up in her eyes. "I've wanted to see you. But Hugh said—"

"Damn Hugh! Where is he?"

"I don't know," chokingly. "That's why I came here. We've been out on a homestead beyond the Cross Anchor. Hugh said if I'd stay there with him until summer . . . give him another chance . . . he would give me a divorce." She flushed. Her eyes fell. "Honest, Grey, I've tried so hard. I guess . . . you'll never understand."

"I guess I won't," he said coldly. "You loved Barrington. And I was fool enough to love you . . . a nice . . ."

Something in her widened eyes stopped him. She faced him for a moment, lips quivering, tears bubbling down on her cheeks. Then, whirling, she ran outside. He stood looking after her for a moment, turned to face Brown.

"Howdy, Sage." There was no welcome in the usually cordial voice of the secretary. "You've got no business talking to her that way. She's been eating her soul out for you. She didn't know what the rest of us knew. We didn't have the heart to tell her. After all, you're a married man. You still have a wife who is probably having just as tough a time of it as you have had."

"You . . . mean . . . Alice?"

"Yes. She threw Mortimer over—made him get off the Cross Anchor. She undertook to run it herself. She brought Judy in to-day. She'll be back here in a few minutes."

Grey glanced about fearfully.

"And Judy really tried to find me?"

"She didn't know anything about your getting hurt, I tell you. Barrington got her away by\ lying. But . . . it's none of my affair."

"Judy!" Grey breathed.

"We fellows wouldn't tell her. We wanted to spare her if you didn't get well. We thought you wouldn't want her to know you'd never ride again."

"But Barrington?"

"Came to town about a month ago. Put on a big drunk—the first he'd had for weeks. Got to shooting off his head, disappeared. Judy stuck on the place out there in the mountains until she nearly starved. Alice found her, brought her to the Cross Anchor. She was pretty sick for a time. Kept begging them to let her die. She finally pulled through in spite of herself. Came to town to-day to hunt Barrington, hoping for word from you."

"But you don't understand . . ." Grey began angrily.

"Neither do you. It's none of my business, but there's no reason for treating a wonderful woman like Judy Barrington as you just did. Mrs.

Brown and myself know her and Alice better than the rest. That's the reason we take such an interest. We'd give everything to see the smiles back on their faces. Something has happened to Barrington. Judy got some money to-day. It came addressed to her in care of me."

"What was the address?" Grey asked, suddenly ashamed of himself and seeking some way to cover his embarrassment.

"Provo, Wyoming. But what do you care? You just sent Judy out crying—breaking her heart."

"Shut up, or I'll choke the life out of you," Grey snarled. "I'm headed for Provo after Barrington." He glared at Brown, who was regarding him strangely, half fearfully. "Going to choke the life out of him for cracking me up at Arvada . . . and right here in Arapahoe. You might tell Judy or anybody else who asks." He limped away, boot-heels clumping savagely.

Chapter XXVII

The little cow-town of Provo, Wyoming, lay stark in the scorching July sun, silent as a tomb in its afternoon torpor. The huddled, weather-beaten buildings radiated heat like the top of a stove. Heat-waves shimmered upward from the single, hard-packed gumbo street, deserted save for a half-dozen ponies dozing at the hitch-rails, weight on three legs, eyes closed, noses twitching to dislodge the tormenting flies.

The only shelter from the sun was inside the Gold Coast saloon. And Grey Sage had sought it out. He sat tilted back against the wall, listening abstractedly to the conversation of a brush-scarred cowhand and an untidy bar-tender.

"The strangest case we ever heard in Provo," the cowboy was saying. "That ranny confessing a murder . . . just sits there and gives the judge the horse laugh."

"That's contempt of court," the bar-tender said in a tone of judicial thought.

"That's what the prisoner claims." The cow-hand skinned back cracked lips over snaggle teeth in a grin. "He told the judge he'd made a mess of things . . . was guilty as hell . . . wouldn't offer any defence. Why, he even refused to have a lawyer."

"Jeez!"

"But the other walloper in jail with Barrington says—"

Grey Sage's chair came down with a bang. In a half-dozen stiff-legged strides he was across the room, facing the startled pair.

"Did you say Barrington, jasper?" he jerked out. "You ain't by any chance meaning Hugh Barrington?"

"That's what he calls himself." The cowboy backed off. "Know him?"

"Too damned well." Grey slapped his stiff leg. "He gave me this, damn his soul! I'm here to get him."

"You're too late," the puncher said. "He'll swing."

"Fill 'em up." Grey flipped out a coin. The bartender sent a bottle and glasses caroming over. The cowboy poured himself four fingers, swallowed it in a gulp. Grey toyed thoughtfully with his glass.

"So Hugh has confessed to a murder?" Grey's mind was busy—not with thought of Hugh, but of Judy. "What's the low-down?"

"That's what the court is trying to find out." The cowboy poured himself another drink, smacked his lips on it, dashed it off. "Barrington killed a jasper by the name of . . . Harmon, I think it was—John Harmon—down south some-wheres."

"Killed a jasper by the name of Harmon?" Grey was barely conscious that he spoke, yet he shouted in his excitement.

"Confesses it . . . laughs about it . . . begs them to hang him for it. The dangdest thing you ever heard. It's a cinch he did the killing or he wouldn't be bragging . . . unless liquor's got him and he's cracked."

"I don't understand."

"Neither does anybody else. This Harmon must be dead. If he is, he can't talk. Barrington was arrested for fighting here in the Gold Coast. He went plumb off his head from then on. Spilled his guts about the murder."

But Grey Sage waited to hear no more. He left the saloon. It took him but a short time to locate the prosecuting attorney.

"You're wasting your time talking to me," that individual said. "I don't know any more about the case than you do. If there was a murder we'll have to establish a motive . . ."

"But I know the story," Grey interrupted excitedly. "I was tried for that murder. How long will it be before the trial?"

"Thirty days. But he is broke and won't accept public defence. Are you a friend of his?"

"Friend," explosively. "Hell, no . . . I hate his guts. But there is someone . . ." He slammed from the office, leaving the prosecutor staring after him.

So Hugh Barrington had killed John Harmon. He could see it now. Hugh had tried to hurt him at the trial. Hugh's story then had struck him as studied, memorized. But Harmon? He had hated Harmon—worse even than he hated Hugh. But to clear himself he determined to finance the court battle of Hugh Barrington. He would clear himself of the doubt Mason said people still had. He would see that Barrington was convicted . . . or if he was freed he would kill him. Hugh at the moment represented all the trouble he had encountered in his life.

So Barrington had killed Harmon. That accounted for the change in the fellow from the moment they left the Cross Anchor. Hugh had attempted to stifle an accusing conscience with drink. Judy had wondered if there wasn't something on his mind.

A confession by Barrington would have saved him from the ordeal of the trial. Yet he had seen him taken to court and tried for a crime he did not commit. Barrington's testimony had worried Mortimer, had hurt his own chances of escape.

But at least the fellow would have a fair trial, amply financed. He would see to that, for Judy's sake . . . for his own sake, to make certain that Barrington's conviction would for all time remove any doubt as to his own innocence.

But the money. He knew of no living soul. Unless, perhaps Alice—

He rebelled at the thought. He wanted none of her money. He hadn't laid eyes on her for months. But why not get the whole thing out of his system now that the time had come? Why not give her a divorce? She deserved it. She had been a good sport about it all. Brown had said she had broken with Mortimer.

Before he was scarcely aware of what he was doing, he was headed out of Provo for the Cross Anchor, headed for a new chapter in his career that he was never fully able to comprehend—an inextricable maze of bewildering events that left him groggy, only barely conscious of the things that were breaking about him.

But he did not go to the Cross Anchor. He went to Arapahoe instead . . . arrived on the eve of the stampede. It reminded him of another time a year before. Then he had come as a green country boy, unversed in the ways of the world.

Chapter XXVIII

"Ladies and gentlemen!"

The voice of Tom Brown came booming through the megaphone from the judge's stand. "The men's world championship bronc-riding contests. A late entry will interest you. Grey Sage, who last year rode Widow-Maker, but lost the championship on a protest, has entered. He was hurt at the Arvada Stock Show by that same Widow-Maker. Three cheers for Grey Sage. Here he comes out of chute number one on Blackmailer, the toughest horse . . ."

Two things happened with astounding rapidity. Judy Barrington, standing directly beneath the stand, clutched wildly at her breast, took a faltering step, pitched into the arms of a passing bronc-rider. Alice Harmon Sage—a quiet, unostentatious figure in black, far back in the grand-stand—crumpled into the lap of a man beside her who set up a hue and a cry that rivaled the commotion that greeted Grey's own ride.

Grey Sage aboard Blackmailer hit the hard-packed arena with a resounding thud.

Alice, in a complete state of collapse, was carried out and taken away in an ambulance. When Judy again gained possession of her faculties, clouds of dust defied sight in the arena, rocked with thunderous applause.

Through a maze of reeling wits, she heard the pick-up gun. A mighty shout led her to believe that Grey Sage had come back . . . one of the very few. The bellow of the announcer jerked her from a consuming lethargy.

"And now for the ladies' world bronc-riding championship. Introducing Judy Barrington, one of the greatest riders of all times. And, ladies and gentlemen, I am sorry to announce that Grey Sage has been badly hurt."

The rest was lost on Judy as she ran blindly towards the chutes.

Grey hurt . . . hospital bills. Brown had told her of his misfortune. Her mind was in a tempest. She had paid her debt to Hugh. Now it was her own happiness, her happiness and Grey Sage's, that counted.

Scarcely knowing what she was about, she climbed the chutes. To her mind flashed a vision. That day they had met there in the barn at the Cross Anchor. She recalled with startling detail every word of their conversation. That day had marked the beginning of things for her, had changed her whole life.

Then she had settled herself in the saddle aboard a raw-boned sorrel, sat close-penned, looking down a bowed and muscular neck at plastered, twitching ears. Seconds seemed eternities. Through her mind tumbled everything Barrington had told her. Hugh! She wondered where he was, what he was doing. How strangely everything had turned out. But Grey . . . he was hurt.

The gate swung open. She was in the middle of a whirling dervish that threatened to split her in two. She rode mechanically, as Hugh had taught her, her graceful body glued to the saddle, her quick brain anticipating every move of the crazed brute beneath her. Gone was all reckoning of time. She was barely conscious of thunderous applause. All she knew was that the horse was not her equal . . . that she had ridden many worse . . . that Grey Sage . . . Hugh . . .

Somewhere out of the mad maze behind popped the pick-up gun. A rough arm encircled her waist. She let go all holds, swung over into the saddle of the pick-up man. Her own mount bawled and pitched away across the arena, halter rope flying, stirrups flapping. Then, above tumultuous shouts, she heard her name.

"Judy Barrington wins day money in the ladies' bronc-riding contest!"

She shook herself free of the restraining arm, slid to the ground. Then she was gone across the arena, blindly.

In the farrier's tent she found Grey stretched on a cot. He looked up groggily at her entrance. A pitiful, hopeful light flamed into his pain-wracked eyes.

"Judy!" he murmured brokenly. "I . . . fell down. I . . . made my ride. I won top money. But they say I can't go on. I broke . . . that kidney loose again . . . the doctor in Arvada warned . . . God . . . Judy."

She threw herself on her knees beside him.

"What do we care, Grey?" she cried. "I'll win the woman's championship. I took day money—five hundred dollars. We'll quit—I'll go away with you now, anywhere, where we can forget."

"Mebbeso . . . never . . . now," he gasped. "Judy . . . I rode for you to-day . . . and for Hugh."

"Hugh?" The name was a startled cry on her lips.

"He's up in Provo . . . confessed . . . murder . . ." His words came painfully, almost incoherently. "Much as I hate him, damn him, for our sake I tried to get money to fight—

"Hugh killed John Harmon. Go to Provo, Judy. Save him if you can. Not that I care. But for your sake . . . so he'll know we've always been on the square with him. I've hired Judge Beasley of Arapahoe to fight for him. While you're gone, I'll . . ." His eyelids fluttered, closed.

Judy sprang up.

"Doctor!" she screamed. "He's dead."

"Just pain, my dear." The doctor came in to feel the racing pulse. "He was warned in Arvada never to ride again. As soon as the ambulance comes we'll take him to the hospital. It may be weeks, months."

"Tell him I'll be back." Judy bolted out. "Tell him to hang on and rattle . . . for me. I'm going to Provo. If he should die . . . if you've lied to me . . . I'll come back and settle with you."

With that she was gone, leaving the doctor staring after her, something of a smile tugging at his lips.

Chapter XXIX

It was a strangely familiar world to which Grey Sage opened his eyes . . . white walls . . . white curtains swaying in a gentle breeze . . . white bed . . . white bed-clothes. He was back again in a hospital. He could tell by the infernal odour that never seemed to have left his nostrils. A white-garbed nurse was bending over him, taking his pulse.

"Pulse normal. That's fine," she flashed him a smile that gave him confidence, a feeling of comfort. "You'll be up before you know it." She arranged a bouquet of flowers on the stand beside him. "A gift. Aren't they beautiful?"

"Who sent them?" he whispered hoarsely.

"I don't know. There was no card. They were delivered a while ago. And the doctor said if you were normal at this checking of the chart you were to have a visitor."

"Who?" The whisper was even hoarser.

"I don't know that either. But I do know you're fit as a fiddle. And—"

A rap came at the door—a timid, low rap that somehow made Grey's nerves spring tight.

"I expect that is your visitor now. Do you feel like seeing whoever it is?"

"Let 'em in," he said weakly.

He closed his eyes for a moment's rest. He seemed to tire so easily. Even talking was an effort. If his brain would just cease its whirling, he would feel so much stronger. It was that constantly whirling brain that tired him so. He wished no one had come. But then . . . he wondered where Judy was. Perhaps his visitor . . .

His eyes flew open, widened, came to rest on the face of Alice—Alice, his wife.

With a little cry the girl came over to the bed, laid a hand over his fingers.

"Forgive me for coming, Grey," she choked. "But I heard you were hurt. I've heard all about everything in the last few days. Too bad I didn't know before . . . about Arvada. I could have helped so much.

"Don't try to talk," she cautioned, sealing his parched lips with a finger as he essayed a reply. "Just rest. You look so pale and tired. Grey, is there anything I can do? Is there anything you want?"

He tried not to look at her. For her eyes were so sincere and sad. He wondered if Alice, too, hadn't gone through much since they last met.

"If you care to . . ." he found himself whispering, "you might help Judy fight for Hugh. He confessed killing your uncle, you know."

"I didn't know!" Her hand flew to her breast. "But I do remember now. I passed Hugh Barrington in the hall just outside the door as I left Uncle

John that night. And Uncle John was going to let him go as foreman. Oh, why couldn't we have seen this before? How different things might have been! Hugh and Uncle had words. Hugh had been drinking . . . it's all so plain now . . . and no one ever suspected him. I'll take care of it, Grey."

He blinked. There were tears in her eyes that had lost that coldness. She was stunning in black. Never before had he seen her so beautiful. And she was . . . but it was too late for that now. They had drifted too far apart. She never had meant anything to him. It always had been Judy. . . .

He couldn't think. He didn't feel equal to the effort. After all, what was the use?

"You didn't . . . want to marry Mortimer?" he jerked out.

She shook her head.

"No . . . after you left . . ." She bit her lip. "But never mind, Grey. I just don't want you to think the things I know you have thought. It's all over now. Why be bitter about it?"

His other hand had found hers.

"I'm not bitter . . . at anything or anybody, Alice. Hugh up there in jail . . . I went up to kill him. He crippled me in Arapahoe . . . because I . . . but now . . . I see things so differently. . . . Seem to feel . . ."

"I know how you feel," she cut in on him quietly. "I feel that way too, Grey. There was a time . . . I wish, however, you would let me do something for you. I have so much, Grey. It means nothing to me. Won't you, please?"

"You can do something with your money, Alice," he said slowly. "Something that every cowboy in the country will thank you for to their dying day. Start a fund for a home for cowboys crippled in the rodeo arena. Take care of the bronc-riders who hobble about, unable to work simply because they were game enough to keep the thousands cheering at their dangerous sport. Alice, will you do that?"

Her eyes sparkled delightedly.

"I'll start it immediately," she cried, almost gaily, he thought. "I'll put the thing before Tom Brown. I'll start it with a million if necessary, just for the bronc-riders and contestants who are actually hurt beyond help in the rodeos. Oh, Grey, it's a wonderful idea—something I've wanted to do all my life. As quickly as you are able, won't you work with me, help me with this thing?"

He looked at her strangely.

"Are you asking me . . . to help you?" he repeated uncomprehending.

"Yes, Grey. I've always wanted you to help me. But somehow we just didn't get started right. I loved you, Grey, no matter what has occurred since that night. I have loved you from the first . . . and . . . I still love you."

She dropped her head on his hand, nestled it against her flaming cheek.

"But I'm not here asking for anything. Grey, I've found something out of this almost unbearable loneliness. I've found peace."

"You . . . care . . . that . . . much?"

She gazed at him with tear-dimmed eyes.

"I'll never care for any one again as I care for you, Grey. The night you left, Mortimer also went."

"You sent him away! And you—"

"That doesn't matter. When you walked out I knew he meant nothing. Grey, I didn't want to tell you this—it isn't what I came for. I just had to see you again before—"

"Before what?"

"I'm flying East to-night. There's some business. But I'll make it a point to get your cowboys' home foundation started before I go. And I'll make you a trustee." She got to her feet, collected herself. Again she was the Alice Harmon he had known and feared, composed and cool. "I'll be going along now. Don't worry. Everything is taken care of here. And, Grey, please, promise me one thing. If you should . . . won't you, please, for the love I know you felt for me . . . won't you please let me help you?"

He shook his head.

"All right," she sighed. "Then I'll be going . . . and see about your cowboys' home. After that

I'll take off. I'll be gone until fall. Then, Grey, the way is open if Hugh has confessed. Judy can get a divorce. Do you want me to . . . start an action? I can now. I realize that you were too much of a man to do it. Thank you, Grey, from the bottom of my heart. Judy told me . . . it was so noble and big. I didn't deserve it. But now . . . a year has elapsed. We can make the separation legal on the grounds of desertion."

"Let's don't talk about it now," he said wearily. "It's caused so many heartaches already. Forget it until you come back, anyway. Then we can go over it. I don't want to hurt anybody any more. We've all been so blind, and we've hurt each other so."

She stooped and kissed him on the lips. He closed his eyes. That kiss carried more meaning than any other he had had in his life save one—the kiss of Judy Barrington that night at the Cross Anchor.

Judy and Alice! He opened his eyes. Alice was gone.

Chapter XXX

"Air-Liner Crashes! Twelve Perish in Flames!"

The newspapers carried the story in glaring headlines. But to Grey Sage, lying in the hospital at Arapahoe, no word was given of the tragedy. Nor for almost a month did he know. Then it was as he was leaving the hospital, his hair almost snow-white, his once tanned and wind-whipped face lean and gaunt.

In the outer office the doctor told him of the crash, handed him a packet. Alice had left it for him the day he had last seen her.

He stumbled blindly from the hospital, out into the fresh air.

Alice—the girl he had married—dead! Alice had walked from that lingering kiss to her doom.

The world seemed suddenly tumbling down about him. He opened the packet with trembling fingers. Not even after he had scanned through it did he realize its contents. It was a copy of a will. It left everything to him—him, Grey Sage, a millionaire.

But he didn't care. It meant nothing. He had loved Alice in his own peculiar way. He had really worshipped her in a strange manner. She had been something of an untouchable goddess, and now—

He stumbled out to the curb. He turned to look back. The doctor was watching him closely. And the car just ahead. From it bounded a little figure. That figure was in his arms. He was moaning, barely conscious of repeating her name over and over again. And she was doing the same thing.

"Judy . . . Judy . . . Judy!"

"Grey . . . Grey . . . Grey!"

It seemed as though he never wanted to let her go. Somehow he knew that she was his now, that never again would they be separated.

She was helping him into the car. He recognized the driver. One of the men from the Cross Anchor. And the car was the Harmon limousine. But he paid no heed. He was aching for this girl cuddled beside him, who had drawn his head over on her shoulder, was stroking his throbbing temples with a tenderness that made him drowsy. He was so tired all of a sudden. Nothing mattered now . . . just so this strange dream was not interrupted.

The car was in motion. Still he could not move under this spell, couldn't move until warm, moist lips found his. He started up suddenly, as though an electric current had been plunged through his body. He looked at the girl beside him. She hadn't changed so much. There were fine lines of worry at the corners of her eyes. She still had about her that fresh and healthy glow that made him love her. And her strong arms were crushing him, clinging to him hungrily.

"Hugh," he managed to whisper in a strange unnatural voice.

"He . . . he," she faltered. ". . . oh, Grey, it's all too horrible that it had to end this way . . . that we should find our happiness through the misfortunes of others. But, we have each other, dear. And we're going home. Alice gave me the Cross Anchor. After all, she was so good. I did love her."

"I know," he murmured. "She came to see me that day she left. But, Judy, instead of going to the Cross Anchor, couldn't we go back and see old Mason—just you and me? Go back on the Cheyenne River and my homestead? The house isn't much. But it will be peaceful and happy up there—with you."

"Anywhere, dear . . . just so I'm with you," she whispered.

Another Indian summer in the Rockies. Hazy, lazy days filled with listless hours—cattle grazing on dun-coloured flats, a slow wind whining across the prairies, water-holes glistening blindly, the bawl of a steer here, the answering bawl of a steer there. Peace, quiet, awesome vastness, broken only by the whir of grasshoppers, the shrill of locusts.

Out on the purple skyline rode two riders. One sprang lithely from the saddle. The other climbed down stiffly. Then they were seated beside each other, holding hands.

"Don't fret, Grey darling," Judy begged. "Everything will be all right—now that we have each other."

"But you're the woman bronc-riding champion," he said huskily. "All my life I've dreamed of being a champion."

"You're a champion through me," she said softly, her fingers running through his hair. "Don't you see? First it was Harmon, then it was Hugh who kept you from winning. Hugh told me before he . . . he did swing that gate against your leg at Arapahoe, and at Arvada."

A scowl clouded his face. But it vanished under the caress of her fingers.

"The first time it was to win a championship; the second it was jealousy, Grey. He hated you because of me. But he loved you as a man. . . ." Tears fell unheeded across her cheeks. "Then, when I went to see him in that Provo jail—after he'd been convicted—they'd found him . . . dead."

"Never mind, honey," Grey's hand closed over hers. "I'll make it up to you. We love this place, like old Mason said I would if I ever got the right woman—a woman of the West. Dreams aren't everything. We'll farm if we feel like it. I'll just let my wife be the champion for the whole family."

"Your wife . . . God love you, Grey Sage.

You've won a greater championship than the world can bestow—the championship of manhood. You risked your life to raise money for the defence of Hugh, who'd injured you, crippled you, blasted your lifelong dreams. Don't you remember what that Bible says, honey?—'For greater love hath no man than . . .'

"Championship! Me riding out there and taking first money . . . every jump they make I jab them for you, darling . . . for you. I'm not the champion you are, because I quit several times, laid down and let you worry about us, knowing that some day you would find a way out for us."

He sighed, pillowed his head in her encircling arms, drew one stiff leg to an easier position. That sigh whitened his lips.

"Mebbeso, dear," he whispered huskily. "It's a hell of a game that makes cripples of us for the entertainment of the howling mobs. But now, thanks to Alice, we've got that home started. It's worth while, Judy—now that I've found you. And while I'm here, I'm going to find what happiness there is left . . . here in your arms . . . with you . . . Judy."

About the Author

Francis W. Hilton was born in Lexington, Nebraska, but at two years of age moved with his family to Newcastle, Wyoming, where his father worked for the *Newcastle News-Journal*, a newspaper he eventually bought. Newspaper journalism was in Hilton's blood, and after attending a year at the University of Michigan he returned to Newcastle where he worked for his father. In Newcastle, Hilton covered the sheriff's office and got to know several prisoners who told him stories of the old West in the days of cattle wars and outlaws. These stories inspired his ambition to write Western fiction, which he began publishing in the 1920s in such pulps as *Western Story Magazine*, *Frontier Stories*, and *Lariat Story Magazine*. Beginning with *Phantom Rustlers* in 1934, Hilton branched out into writing Western novels. Some of these such as *Long Rope* (1935) were expansions of short stories that had earlier appeared in magazines. In most of Hilton's stories, there are elements of mystery and detection, thus combining one popular genre with another. Hilton's descriptions of Western terrain and natural occurrences such as cloudbursts are extremely vivid and unforgettable. In the 1940s, while still writing Western fiction for the magazine market, Hilton continued working for various local newspapers as a writer and editor, and in 1947 founded the *Columbia Basin News* in the state of Washington. In the 1950s, Hilton bought a magazine intended for vegetarians, and helped by his wife, published it until he retired in 1959. His last days found him living again in Newcastle. His reputation as a Western author rests primarily on the ten novels he wrote, many of which were subsequently published in paperback editions, and all of which, in Hilton's words, provide a whiff of something "that reminded me of sagebrush."

Center Point Large Print
600 Brooks Road / PO Box 1
Thorndike, ME 04986-0001 USA

(207) 568-3717

US & Canada:
1 800 929-9108
www.centerpointlargeprint.com